Torn

True Love

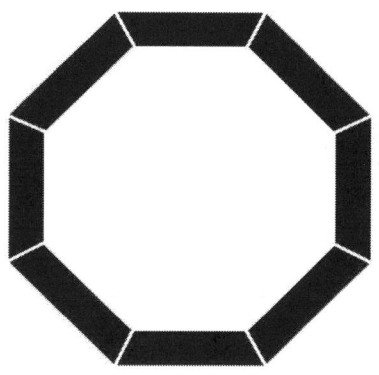

By KD Ferguson

Copyright © 2014 KD Ferguson

Published by Anchor Group Publishing

PO Box 551

Flushing, MI 48433

Anchorgrouppublishing.com

Map Design by Garrett Brignoli

Edited by Melanie Williams

All rights reserved. Published by Anchor Group. No part of this book may be reproduced or transmitted in any form or by any means, electronic or mechanical, including photocopying, recording, or by any information storage and retrieval system, without written permission from the publisher.

Dedication

To my husband who puts up with incessant writing, which leads to a lack of attention.

Your love and support means everything to me.

An enormous thank you to Garrett Brignoli for the drawing of my new world. You were able to pull the image from my head and perfectly put it on paper, you're so amazingly talented.

I couldn't have done this without the encouragement of so many.

This is for everyone who supported me on this long journey.

Thank you for believing in me.

~May you never feel torn.~

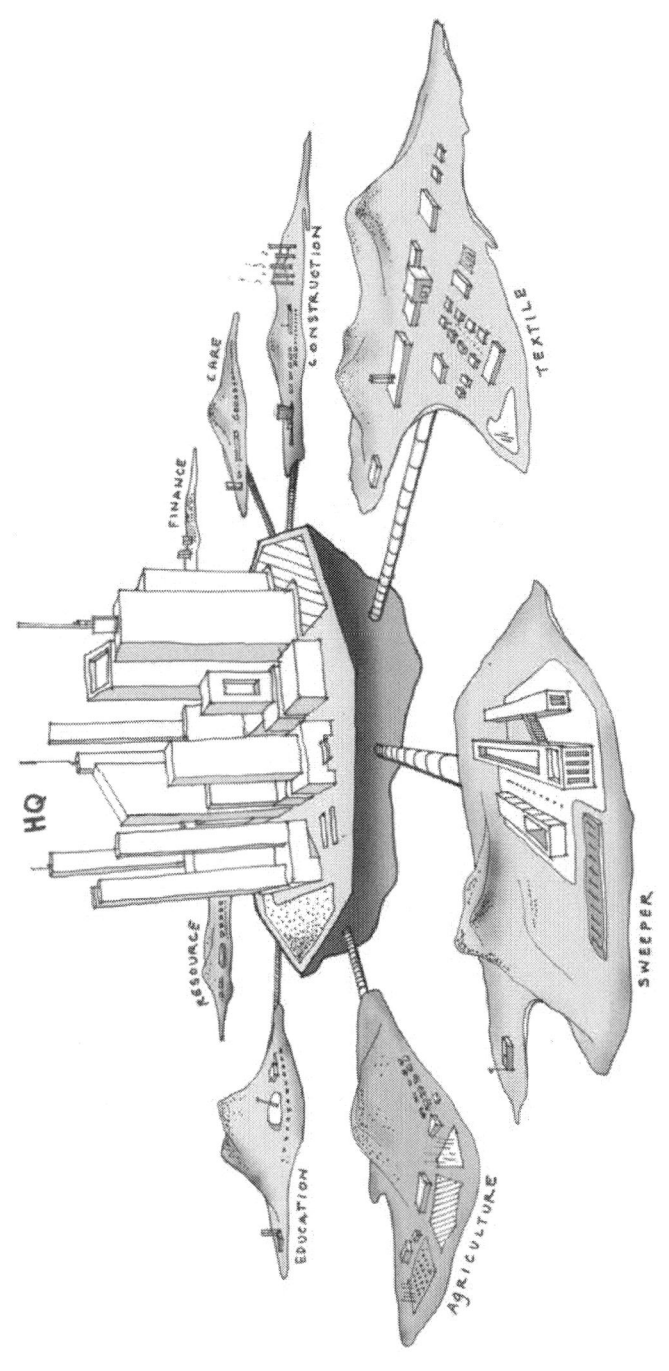

Prologue

I wanted to believe in true love,
Because I truly loved *him*.
My love was more than he deserved.
Discontent filled me,
But I forced myself to believe this was happiness.
The title *True Love* felt so deceptive.
Betrayal, deceit and torment tainted my affection.
How could our love have been so genuine if it was never honest?
This love didn't feel pure and simple,
Rather, it was difficult and pained with emotions.
True love for me was malicious and spiteful,
Hurting like an open wound filled with salt.
Another Band-Aid, it would be fine;
But how many Band-Aids would I apply?
How many lies would I have to tell myself before reality appeared?
If all of Braiden's being was a lie,
I never wanted to accept the truth.

One

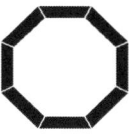

"Hurry up, Joy," I said. "We're gonna miss the whole first half!"

"Relax, Krissa. They never start on time. We'll be fine," Joy replied as we pulled into the parking lot. Our high school girls' soccer team was playing their first game of the season. I always tried to attend the games to support Honor, who was my best friend, a starting mid-fielder and Hope, who was like a sister to me, a starting defender. After ten years of playing soccer, this year was the first year I wasn't on the team; I was burnt out. My parents were disappointed, but I had to do what was right for me.

Our town was small but quaint. Like all of the other surrounding units, we had a population of approximately thirteen thousand and were regulated by the government. My unit was located north of Headquarters, and our community was required to supply all textiles, clothing, fabrics and hard goods, to our sister units. We had seven neighboring units, all of which were responsible for their own specific production—which were assigned by the government—to help support our country as a whole. Shaped similarly to an octagon, Headquarters resided in the middle with entrances and exits leading into each unit.

It's still strange to call it a country, considering the downsizing of the land. A world that was once vast and seemed endless was now small and inadequate in comparison. After all the fighting, disease, pollution and the havoc Mother Nature created for us, we weren't left with much. But the system in place now is great, our government restored us, and we've been taught how to adapt; what happened in the past won't happen again.

The system developed after the war demolished most of what used to be known as the United States. As far as we know, we're all that's left. Our Headquarters took over after the fall and rebuilt us to what we are now. Headquarters is now our government, controlling all the units so that we run in a successful, peaceful manner. Living by their rules and guidelines, every citizen has a home and staples to live a healthy, average life. We receive what we need but have the ability to upgrade our material possessions by training hard, landing a great job and earning good money.

The rolling hills of the textile unit were beautiful in the fall, our spring and summer months were nice, but the winters seemed endless and left something to be desired. I lived in the kind of place where you'd let your kids ride their bikes in the neighborhood without worrying, happy marriages existed without much divorce, and people spoke to their neighbors and attended each other's BBQs. There was a sense of familiarity and security in our town, but I knew a long time ago this wasn't the place for me. I wanted more. The mom and pop shops and restaurants along Main Street were nice, but limiting, with nothing to do on the weekends. After seventeen years, the city where I grew up had become dull and boring. I wanted to be in a place that was exciting; one filled with endless possibilities.

I was a girl with big dreams. That's why my plan was to go to Headquarters after graduation. The population there was much larger with more opportunities for work, and to be honest, I was ready for a change. At the end of senior year, each student from every unit was given the chance to rank his or her desired unit, and Headquarters tried to accommodate everyone's number one choice. The Enforcers decided where we'd each go by looking at personal preference, the ability to gain work in a given field, basic supply and demand, and compliance with the government's rules and regulations. The better your behavior, the more likely you were to be placed in your top pick.

When we took a school trip to Headquarters, I was in awe. Before venturing into high school, each student—excluding the Sweeper unit—toured the country to learn about our government and see how each unit runs and operates. I knew after graduation, I would be Center bound because the seven other units did not appeal to me. Sure, I'd miss my family, but we could always visit. I really wanted to see more than what our textile unit offered.

"Joy, can you believe we're seniors? It's so wild to think this is our last year of high school! This is going to be the best ever.

Homecoming, graduation, senior prom! Ugh, who am I going to go to all the dances with this year? I really have no interest in anyone right now," I said, already worrying about the social events in the upcoming year.

It was more than that though. I knew pairing would be coming up soon. Not only did we get to choose our unit, but we were also able to choose our mate. When the country rebuilt, our government thought it would be in everyone's best interest to be *paired* with a life-long mate. Apparently in the old days, many relationships ended in divorce, which resulted in battles over children—not to mention conflicts over lovers who were supposedly spoken for. A lot of violence and destruction occurred due to love, or the lack there of. Therefore, the Enforcers have regulated marriages and given us some choice, which has helped keep the peace.

The government begins pairing each *single* after he or she generates a list of potential mates their senior year. A typical list is made up of individuals you've grown up with, but I never envisioned my list to be typical.

"Why don't you just ask Chance?" Joy asked in a joking manner while she unnecessarily checked herself out in the visor mirror one last time before we stepped out of the car. Joy was flawlessly beautiful. She had long dark hair and stunning green eyes. Her skin was tan all year long and matched, if not exceeded, that of the models in commercials. This made the rest of us quite jealous. I didn't need the mirror. My eyes were still hazel, my brown hair, mostly covered with blonde highlights, was still pin straight.

"Yeah, right. We're so over. I've grown so tired of all the games and need to move on." That statement was true; I just wasn't sure how to *move on*. Would anyone be able to fill the shoes Chance no longer wanted to wear? For certain he was wrong for me, but I still had a hard time letting go.

"True. You can do better anyways."

"I know. It was fun while it lasted, but it's time to move on to bigger and better things, if I *can* find bigger and better." My mind had no problem with the words I was saying, but my heart still ached a little when they came out. Being picky when it came to guys, there were plenty that were interested, but the feelings weren't mutual.

"Well, he can always be your back-up plan," Joy pointed out.

"Very true." After all, I'd played that part for so long now, it'd only be fair to let him see how it felt.

As we walked up the bleachers to watch the game, we passed Chance, my boyfriend from a year ago and most recently my summer fling. I guess you'd call him my first *real* boyfriend. Chance was the boy who stole a lot of my *firsts*. Although I dated before he came along, it was casual. When I met Chance I wanted it to be serious, so I made the decision, or the mistake, that he'd be the one to whom I'd lose my virginity. Maybe that's why I was so entranced with him and found it so difficult to move on. Having sex was a big deal to me. Although I wanted my first time to be meaningful, I never thought I'd wait until my pairing ceremony night. I wasn't the type to go out and lay down for just anyone. My first time with Chance wasn't anything amazing, but it felt right, and at the time I was glad that I decided to do it. It was the aftermath that tainted it all. I didn't feel special anymore and believed he thought the same of me, given the way he treated me.

Unexpectedly, Chance cheated on me, and to everyone's shock, I took him back. My friends all said I was too good for him, but I was stupid. I just wasn't ready to give him up. After cheating on me a second time, he broke all ties and left me for her.

When Chance and I started dating, I really thought he had potential. I considered a future with him, but after our tremulous relationship, my friends were right, it could never work. He didn't take anything seriously and had pushed me aside for a girl that didn't have much going for her. If that was what he really wanted then we certainly weren't right for one another. Besides, he wasn't going to pair, and there was no way I was going to end up becoming a Sweeper.

Being a Sweeper was basically a death sentence, it was the lowest unit in our society. They held the lowest jobs, which required little to no education, and none of the work at that level provided a good quality of life. Sweepers were placed due to being unpaired or resisting the government. Apparently Headquarters believed you did not have a lot of worth if you were unable to pair and reproduce. Reproduction was vital to keeping our society alive and thriving. If an individual didn't see it that way, they were put to use, cleaning up after the rest of us. And while I'd never actually visited the Sweeper unit, I'd heard enough about the land and people living there to know I wanted to stay far away from it. With Chance out of the picture, I knew I deserved better and was certain I could find it.

I needed something more concrete. I only had two years left until I was permanently paired, and by the end of the year, I needed to provide a preliminary list.

I was stressed but still believed in the process. In the next two years I knew I would find and be paired with my true love.

"How's it going, Kris?" Chance asked, trying to act cool in front of his friends as Joy and I took seats several benches higher than them.

"I'm fine. How are you guys?" The four of them—Chance, Tobin, Pax, and Braiden—didn't look like the type to be friends. Chance wore his signature look of layered shirts with a twisted rope necklace around his neck. Wearing a blue polo and khakis, Tobin had a more reserved, conservative look. Pax was a small kid with dark hair and brown eyes who wore sweatpants and an old T-shirt, but then ... there was Braiden. Braiden had dark short hair, striking green eyes and a well-defined jaw. His face was long and oval, beautiful yet rugged, and had a look that stole my attention away from all other things.

Chance and Braiden had been friends for a long time. Chance used to always talk about him when we were together, and I had seen Braiden on several occasions but I never really paid attention. Paying no attention to any other male prospects, I only saw Chance. Today, however, was different. For the first time, I *saw* Braiden. There was something different about him now. His smile or his laugh, something drew my attention.

"Krissa? Are you going to answer me?" Braiden asked. My thoughts were interrupted by the sound of his voice.

"I'm sorry, Braiden, what did you ask?"

"How's your health project coming along?" Occasionally we crossed each other's paths as he left health and I entered.

"I'm trying to finish up the research part, so I can finally start the paper."

"I actually picked a topic I enjoy learning about."

"Oh yeah, what's that?" I asked, trying to keep the conversation going.

"Teenage drug abuse, ha-ha."

"Like you really need to do much research about that," I told him, knowing of several instances where he and Chance had taken part in getting high.

"Yeah, yeah."

We continued to talk about mindless subjects until Joy interrupted, claiming she was thirsty. "Hey, Krissa, go with me to get something to drink?"

"All right. Later guys," I said as Joy and I walked to the concession stand.

We made our way toward the brick concession stand

building, and I could feel Joy's eyes burning into my back as I walked. "What was that about?" Joy abruptly asked.

"What?" I asked, turning around to meet her stare.

"You're not thinking the whole break-up with Chance was a bad idea, are you? Please tell me you don't want him back."

"No. I was just spacing out. You know, thinking about school work and what not." I knew she didn't believe me, but I'd rather her think I was focused on Chance rather than Braiden. By the time she placed her order and we were walking back to a different section of the bleachers, we'd moved on to a topic Joy was interested in, her crush, Gabriel.

After the game was over and Joy had driven me home, I convinced myself my thoughts about Braiden were a moment of weakness. Going to bed that night with a clear conscience and a bright outlook on the year ahead of me, I had no idea my life had started down a path that would drastically change my future.

The next day at school was anything but typical. Everyone was pumped about the homecoming dance that upcoming weekend and looking forward to the first football game of the season. The opening half-time show was being performed by the dance team, which my best friend, Honor, and I co-captained.

The last bell rang, and the halls were swarmed with kids. I found Joy first, and we headed toward the doors. Before we could reach the exit, Braiden and Chance stopped us.

"What up, Kris?" Chance asked, trying to appear casual.

"Just ready to head home. What are you guys up to?"

"Ah, nothing. Braiden just had something to ask you," he told me as he nudged Braiden closer to where I stood.

"Okay," I said, not really understanding what was going on.

"So um," Braiden started to say. "There's this thing people go to, together …"

"Uh huh," I said confused, looking around at the sea of students flooding the front doors and wondering if any of them were paying attention to our random conversation.

"Where they dance and stuff," Braiden said with a bit of confidence combined with a strange awkwardness.

"Huh? I have no idea what you're talking about, Braiden." I said, shifting uncomfortably, trying to balance my textbooks and book bag.

"Krissa, he's trying to ask you to homecoming!" Joy interrupted.

"Oh," I said.

"You should go, Kris. You guys would have fun," Chance encouraged.

I was baffled at how easy it was for him to let me go. Sure, there wasn't a future for us, but that didn't mean I would pass him off to *my* friend. The bitter side of me wanted to accept Braiden's invitation in spite of Chance, but I was also pleasantly surprised by how flattered and excited I was at his offer.

"Um, sure, I'll go with you. Chance is right, we'll have fun," I said to Braiden, all the while glaring at Chance. Maybe Braiden was exactly what I needed.

Two

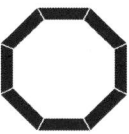

Following Braiden's proposal, I took the initiative to call him. Just dialing my communicator made me nervous, not really sure what to expect. I couldn't help but think maybe this whole thing was a joke, and I was the butt end. But, after talking to Braiden, my nerves were put to ease. He seemed genuinely excited to go to the dance; still, I had my reservations. Everything seemed great thus far, but what if I fell for him and he turned out just like Chance? They were friends after all; maybe he too was a player. I knew I was over thinking, but guarding myself was at the front of my mind.

The week passed quickly. Our football team was playing our rival from the Agriculture unit, and I was jittery about our first performance. Honor and I were excited to show off our team. Considering it was my one and only extra-curricular activity, I took on most of the work. My biggest hope was that the team would help my chances of getting placed at Headquarters, showing my leadership capabilities, dedication and drive.

Everyone knew the team rested on my shoulders, and I

wanted them to be impressed, including Braiden. The first half of the game passed by too quickly, and before I knew it, Honor and I were nervously leading our team to the fifty-yard line. We lined up in our beginning formation and waited for our upbeat music to pour out of the stadium speakers.

Our three-minute routine felt like it took only seconds, ending far too quickly. It finally felt like the long days of choreographing and teaching was all worth it. The overwhelming applause we received afterward let us know our performance was a success.

I couldn't help but wonder if Braiden had made it to see the show. I was nervous to hear what he thought of us, of me. What if he didn't like what he saw? I weaved in and out of the crowd toward the stairs that led to the concession stand. When I reached the top of the stairs, Braiden was waiting for me, just as he said he'd be, looking amazing in a tight fitting t-shirt and jeans.

"You guys were really good, especially the blonde haired girl in the front." He leaned into me. "I'd really like to get to know her," he said in a flirty, playful tone.

I grinned and gave him a playful punch to the shoulder. "Thanks. I might be able to arrange that for you. Thanks for coming."

"I wouldn't miss it."

I smiled and led him down the metal bleachers taking a seat next to my friends. While Braiden and I watched the remainder of the game together, my friends watched us. Surely they were wondering what was happening with Braiden and me. My attention should've been on the field below, but I couldn't stop wondering what really was going on between us.

It was hard to try and hold a conversation during the game, but every so often I'd glance up and catch Braiden's emerald eyes gazing into mine. After our win, the stadium turned into a mass frenzy of screaming fans. Disappointed with our short good-bye, I was optimistic about the following day.

Saturday seemed to drag on. I couldn't wait to get out of dance class so I could begin preparing for the night's festivities. Nails, hair and a chemical bronzer application, I wanted to look exceptional. Not only was I trying to impress my date, I also wanted to make Chance a little jealous, for him to take notice of what he was missing.

Hope was as close to a sister as I would ever get. We grew up across the street from one another and had been inseparable since birth. As such, we decided to go out to dinner together with just our dates.

Hope had been dating Noble, our star football quarterback, for a few months. They were perfect for each other. She was the typical blonde bombshell, while he was the tan, good-looking, muscular All-American boy.

Getting to Braiden's house was pretty simple, even if it was completely out of my way. Braiden lived on the outskirts of town, the complete opposite end from where I lived. I pulled onto his street and began to feel a little queasy. I knew it was only a dance, but I was thinking about the future beyond that. What would his parents think of me? What if they didn't like me? What if *he* didn't like me? Was I setting myself up for another failed relationship? I didn't have time to contemplate that for long because before I could even put my car in park, Braiden was out of his house walking toward me. He opened the passenger side door to my two-door standard government issued car and jumped in.

"Hey." I said, grinning. He smelled incredible.

"Hi."

"Don't you want me to come in? Maybe meet your parents?"

"They're not home tonight."

"Oh," I said, semi-disappointed. Everything felt more official when you met the parents. I put the car in reverse, and we rode a while in silence.

"Thanks for picking me up," he said leaning over and catching my eye.

"No problem."

Everyone was issued the same car by the government two months prior to his or her eighteenth birthday. Considering he wasn't eligible for a car yet, I was the one in the driver's seat.

"You look really nice tonight," he said complimenting my attire, a purple strapless dress that stopped just above the knee, showing off my legs.

"Thank you. You clean up pretty well yourself." He looked great in his grey dress pants, crisp white button down shirt and argyle sweater vest. His smell was intoxicating, and that smile of his, well, it was more of a smirk, kept my focus only on him. I wasn't thinking about anything but us.

We made the short drive to the restaurant where Hope and Noble were waiting for us.

"Great game last night," I told Noble.

"Yeah, nice pass at the end to win it," Braiden chimed in.

"Thanks," Noble replied with gratitude. "I didn't get to see you guys perform, Krissa, but Hope said it was awesome."

"It was. It felt so good to finally get out there, and I'm just glad it all went well."

Conversations continued to flow effortlessly throughout our dinner. Noble and Braiden seemed to get along really well, which was nice given Chance hadn't gotten along with any of my friends. Braiden was a breath of fresh air.

"Thanks again for being my wing woman," I said to Hope as she and I walked slightly ahead of the boys on the way to our cars.

"Glad I could help. It seems like you guys did fine together."

"I think it went really well."

"So, you like him?"

"I do."

"Just don't rush it, Krissa."

I appreciated Hope's advice. She was the friend who always offered honesty. To others, her words could come off condescending, but I understood the place she was coming from.

"We'll see you at the dance." She made her way to her car.

"Okay, see you soon." Braiden and I got into the car, but

when I went to pull away, he stopped me.

"I have something for you." He reached into the back seat and pulled a plastic box out from underneath his jacket. Opening up the plastic, he pulled out a beautiful corsage that went perfectly with my dress.

"This is gorgeous, you didn't have to do this," I told him as he slid it on to my wrist.

"I wanted to."

"Thank you so much. It's beautiful."

"It doesn't compare to the way you look tonight." I could feel my cheeks flushing. I smiled.

We reached our small, brick high school at about 9:45, fashionably late considering the dance started at eight o'clock. We got our tickets and made our way to the cafeteria. In the left, front corner of the square room, a DJ was set up and blaring the most popular—government approved—music.

I was hesitant to walk in because I knew all eyes would be on us, being that I was with one of my ex's best friends. No one would have ever put us together. Braiden and I were on different social levels. While I'm all about keeping up appearances, there was something about Braiden I couldn't pass up. He was uniquely beautiful, a diamond in the rough. No polishing needed, he was already brilliant. Until then, he just hadn't been in the right setting; my group of friends intimidated most of the boys in our school, along with any girls who were excluded from our clique. I wasn't proud of this fact, but it was true. I didn't see any point in trying to change the politics of high school. Even though we seemed to be from two different worlds, when we were together, Braiden and I clicked.

We walked on to the dance floor as a slow song began playing. I was right about everyone staring at us, but it didn't matter. I felt as if we were the only two people in the room. He was my only focus. As the song continued to play in the background, I melted into his arms.

"Having fun?" he whispered in my ear.

"Yes, thank you." I scanned the crowd and flinched when I saw Chance's intense stare meet mine. I wasn't sure what to make of it. He was dancing with a girl I hardly knew, and ironically it didn't bother me in the slightest bit. I never expected the day would come that I wasn't jealous or a bit envious of the girl on Chance's arm, but that day had arrived. I had no idea where Braiden and I were headed, but at least I saw a future that didn't include Chance.

As the dance continued on, my friends and I danced to our favorite pop music while Braiden hung out with his friends.

"What's going on between you and Braiden?" Honor asked. We'd been friends since middle school. She was honest, loyal, trustworthy, funny, caring; she was my other half. All my middle school and high school years were memorable and tolerable because of her. "Nothing, we're just having fun."

"I see that." She smiled. She would've been happy to see my with any date I had, as long as it wasn't Chance.

The last slow song began to play, and I found myself being led to the dance floor by Braiden. Listening to the lyrics streaming out of the speakers, I agreed with them wholeheartedly; the vocalist was singing of two young people ready to fall in love. Our bodies moved as one across the dance floor as I thought to myself how appropriate the song was.

The last Homecoming dance I'd ever attend came to an end against my wishes. It wasn't that I was sad it was my last Homecoming; I didn't want my night with Braiden to be over. He grabbed my hand for the first time, interlocking my fingers with his, and I knew he felt the same.

We decided to go back to my house. My parents were pretty laid back, and they wanted to meet my date anyway. We pulled up to my small, quaint house, white ranch with blue shutters—typical three person home in our unit. We got out of my car and made our way through the front door.

"Hey, Mom!"

"Hey, sweetie. How was the dance? Did Honor win homecoming queen?" I answered my mother's questions and introduced her to Braiden.

"Mom, Dad, this is Braiden."

"Nice to meet you, Braiden," my dad said in a fairly intimidating voice as he rudely pushed his way to Braiden. Braiden shook my dad's hand and told him it was nice to meet them both, while trying to avoid my overprotective dad's harsh stares. Standing at a stocky 6'2", my dad could be intimidating.

"You can call me Mr. Channing," he said in his strong voice.

"Well, you can call me Faith, Braiden. It's a pleasure to meet you," my mom said, standing at 5'2" with a petite frame, the polar opposite of my dad. Her light sandy-blonde hair and always-smiling face was far more welcoming than my father's. My mom and dad were an example of a late pairing. My dad grew up in the textile unit, and my mother moved to the same unit after her senior year due to her father's work. Meeting shortly after she moved her training year, they were paired the following year. My dad's family still resided in our unit, whereas my mom's family moved back to the educator unit.

"Same here," Braiden responded.

"We're going to sit on the deck," I told my parents as I led Braiden through my house towards the deck, away from my parents' stares. I grabbed a large blanket off the back of the couch and opened the back door.

"I had a really good time tonight. Thanks for asking me to go with you," I said, taking a seat on a cushioned patio chair.

"You're welcome. I had a nice time, too," he replied, taking the seat next to me.

Placing the warm blanket over my legs, I shared the remaining end with him. We sat in silence for a while until I began to ask some questions about his life. I really knew nothing about him except he was seventeen and he was friends with Chance. He was a little mysterious with his answers, which kept me wanting more.

We spent the first half hour talking about our hobbies, likes and dislikes, and our birthdays. I learned that he was an only child like me and very spoiled. When common questions ran out we went a little deeper.

"Where did your parents go tonight?" I asked.

"My mom and Leon took a trip to another unit to see my mom's sister." The way he answered my question implied Leon was not his biological father, which in return peaked my curiosity. That wasn't common in our community, and I was an inquisitive person; I liked to know the details of people's lives, especially those I hung around.

"So, I take it Leon isn't your dad?" I asked, curious about their relationship. After my words came out, I sensed Braiden's withdrawal. Maybe I was getting too personal. "I'm sorry. You don't have to answer that," I said quickly, trying to retract my question.

"No, it's okay," he said. "My mom and Leon paired when I was two."

"What about your dad?" I continued on with my interrogation, eager to know. It was uncommon for individuals to have a child and not be paired. If a couple had a child together, it was required they be paired together.

"That's something I really don't like to talk about. We'll save that for another time," he said staring up at the clear, starry night.

Braiden's whole demeanor changed after my question. Now he seemed closed off, cold and distant. I tried to bring up other topics, but I'd definitely soured things as our night went from unbelievable to uncomfortable. The night carried on till I finally offered to take him home so we could stay in compliance with the government's 1:30 a.m. curfew, he gladly accepted.

The ride to his house was quiet except for the music from my stereo. When we pulled up to his two-story brick home, I thanked him again for a wonderful night. He kissed me on my cheek and told me he'd call me the next day; I wasn't going to hold my breath.

Three

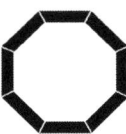

Braiden kept his word, and I was pleasantly surprised when I received a call from him the following day. Surprisingly, it went well. Braiden acted as if our awkward conversation had never taken place. Confused by it all, I decided to leave well enough alone. I figured he'd tell me about his life when he was ready. We moved forward and from that point on, everything fell into place. We waited for each other before school started, went to lunch everyday together and even saw each other every day after school. I felt like I was connecting more with him, putting the pieces of his puzzle together. A month into our relationship, the topic of parents was brought up again, unintentionally, but I figured I'd try again to learn more about his dad.

"Will you ever tell me about your dad?" I asked as I snuggled in closer to him.

He sighed. "Do you believe that when people do bad things, they always go to Hell?" He wrapped the large white blanket tighter around us keeping the November chill out.

His question surprised me for two reasons. One, I wasn't

expecting Braiden to ask such a serious question. He was complicated and difficult to read, but he wasn't a serious person. And two, because he knew I wasn't the religious type. We'd been taught throughout our years of schooling that religion was a huge part of our countries downfall. Our Headquarters allowed religions to exist in each unit, however, if there was any sense of tension, the groups were shut down. Due to the strict regulations, my mom and dad didn't implement religion into my everyday life.

I answered carefully. "I think people make choices that can affect them for the rest of their lives and thereafter. But, I don't think one bad choice, or moment of weakness, dictates where you'll spend eternity. People make bad choices in life, but it doesn't mean they're not sorry, or that they don't regret them. So, no. I don't think a good person who made a mistake, or several mistakes, will automatically go to Hell."

"I was only a year old when my dad left us," Braiden began his story, looking directly up at the sky, "apparently all my parents did was argue. My mom said that her and my dad did nothing but argue. He disagreed with the automatic pairing and no longer wanted to live by Headquarters regulations; believing the rules confined and suffocated who he was as a person, he thought something better was out there for him. She didn't feel restricted and didn't want us to live a sweeper life. My mom worried about what his leaving would do to me, to us. The status of our future was in limbo, but I guess I didn't matter. My mom woke up one morning, and he was gone. He left and never once looked back.

My mom met Leon a year later. Leon's wife passed away unexpectedly in an accident, so Headquarters approved their pairing after considering each of their situations."

"Aren't you curious as to where your dad went?"

"No, if I had to guess I would say the Sweeper unit, but I'm not certain of that," Braiden stated, emotionless.

"Why not? Don't you want closure?"

"Honestly, it's like he's dead to me. My mom and I did just fine without him, so I followed her lead. I want nothing to do with him. He made that choice and didn't want us."

Goose bumps covered my skin. I'd never heard of anyone disobeying Headquarters, and it made me nervous speaking of it. "But maybe he really did. He must have loved you and just didn't like being forced into this lifestyle. Maybe he's in the Sweeper unit."

"Maybe. All I know is I could never leave my family like that, especially my child. I would never be able to turn my back like he did," He said with conviction.

"So you want kids?" I wrapped my arms around his waist a little tighter. Ever since I was a little girl, I'd dreamed of my perfect pairing and my perfect life, which included kids.

"No. I don't think I do."

"Ever?" I asked, surprised at his answer.

He stared me dead in the eye. "I don't see that in *my* future. Nor do I see myself getting paired."

My mind was spinning with a thousand thoughts, but not one

escaped my lips. Granted, we still had time before pairing, but what was the point in us continuing to be together if we both saw our futures so differently? Was I naïve to think we had a future?

"Are you going to say something?" Braiden asked after a long period of silence.

"So you want to remain single?" I avoided eye contact. This conversation was making me very uncomfortable.

"I think so."

"I guess I'm going to be the one who tries to change that outlook then." I really thought maybe I could be the one to change him.

****

I'd completely fallen for Braiden, and while still having reservations about the future, I wanted to move forward. It was hard for me to believe he was going to choose to stay single. We had a great thing going thus far, I couldn't imagine him throwing it away. Months ago I couldn't imagine even talking to another boy except Chance, now I gave him no thought, except for when I had to put up with his interrogations during fitness class fifth period.

"Hey babe," Chance said as I walked out of the locker room dressed for another exciting game of badminton. A while back I would've looked forward to this, spending forty minutes with him, but now, those forty minutes were extremely unpleasant.

"Hi Chance," I said unenthusiastically, "Don't call me babe." I made my way to the basketball court that was set up into four badminton courts.

"Someone's testy today."

"No, I'm fine," I said with attitude. "I just don't like it when you say those kinds of things to me."

"Why not? You used to like it." He handed me a racquet, suggesting I play on his team.

I reluctantly took the racquet, contemplating if I really should put myself in this situation. "Yeah, I liked it back when we were dating, but since we're not anymore, you can drop the affectionate name-calling," I took my place on the court.

"What if I don't want to?" He kept on as our game started.

"What don't you want to do?" I asked, stalling the game.

"Stop."

I didn't need more of an explanation. "You have to," I told him. "You know I'm with Braiden now," I said before serving.

He angrily hit the birdie back over the net. "What if I don't like you guys together?"

"What are you talking about Chance, you're the one who encouraged us to get together, and you're the one who wanted this in the first place," I said while moving quickly out of his way so he could get to the soaring white birdie.

"Well, what if I was wrong? Wrong about the two of you and wrong about us. Why can't we try again? You know, get back together. I miss you, Krissa."

"I'm sorry, what did you just say? I must have misunderstood you." I was in shock.

"You heard me right. I want you back."

"I can't believe you! I can't do this." My shock turned to rage. "You made a choice about us a long time ago, and I'm happy you did. I really like Braiden and want to be with him."

"So what? You don't miss me? You don't ever think about me?" He was smug.

He had no right to want me back. "Not really," I answered.

"Yeah, right."

I knew his ego would have a hard time accepting that. "No, really. I don't think of you like that anymore."

"Well you should. We belong together, Krissa."

"You don't even believe in pairing. We don't stand a chance, we never did." I had been in denial to think we ever did.

"You think you and Braiden do? Good luck with that." He had a point.

I looked around the gym filled with students playing the game. I didn't want to draw any attention to our conversation, but I couldn't help the tone of my voice. "We don't belong together, Chance. And like I said, We. Never. Did," I spat out in disgust. I could handle being friends with him, in fact I wanted to be friends, but not under these conditions.

Class was over, as well as our conversation. I put my racket back and headed for the locker room, not looking back at the mess behind me.

On the way to the only pizza place in town, Nina's, Braiden asked, "How's your day going?"

"Same old stuff, boring classes," I lied, trying to keep my

focus on the road. "You?"

"Same here. Are you sure you're okay? You seem upset," Braiden asked.

"I'm fine. I've got a lot on my mind." I did have a lot buzzing through my brain, but nothing he needed to know about. I knew Braiden was already hesitant about my friendship with Chance and I understood his hesitation about my interactions with Chance. It was an awkward situation, but Braiden had nothing to worry about.

Braiden was so different from anyone else I'd ever spent time with. He was complicated, hard to read, yet easy to be around. He seemed guarded at times and free at others. He built walls around himself for what seemed to be good reasons, but I was willing to try and tear them down. Although I was uncertain about many factors, especially our developing relationship, I was certain about one thing. Braiden was what I wanted.

The remainder of our lunch was uncomplicated. Braiden accepted the fact my mind was discombobulated and dropped the topic. I spent the rest of my time dodging Chance every opportunity I got.

No one had to remind me how unlikely a pairing with Braiden was. I was happy where we were at and optimistic about our future. I knew where I wanted to be and was hoping I wouldn't encounter any obstacles along the way.

Four

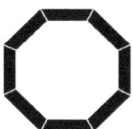

I finally had the opportunity to meet Braiden's parents. It felt long overdue since we'd been together for a few months now, but I was patient while chipping away at Braiden's layers. Knowing I was the first girl he introduced to his family, I convinced myself that had to mean something. I was confident that with enough time spent together, he would most certainly want a future together. A paired life was much more desirable than becoming a Sweeper.

I pulled up to a lavish, two-story traditional brick home on an acre of land lined with tall, slender pine trees. I parked in front of the two-car garage and made my way through the garage toward the entrance to his house where I knocked and waited.

Braiden opened the door and like always, my heartbeat increased. "Hey," I pulled him into a hug.

"Hi, how are you?"

"Good … a little nervous," I said bashfully.

"Don't be nervous, they'll love you," he assured me. He led me through the kitchen and dining room into the living room where his parents sat watching a T.V. program.

"Well hello there, it's nice to finally meet you," said the man getting up from the couch.

"I'm Krissa, it's nice to meet you too," I shook his hand.

"I'm Leon." Leon was tall and slender, with dark hair that was beginning to go grey along the sides. The mustache that met the goatee made him look younger than his mid-forty age.

"Hi, I'm Grace, Braiden's mom." She wasn't what I expected—shorter than me and short blonde hair.

"It's a pleasure to meet you. You have a beautiful home." It was a large, five-bedroom place with all the upgrades one would want. Neutral colors, family pictures and simple décor decorated the space. I didn't expect such an impressive home; most houses in our unit were similar; one-story homes with three or four bedrooms depending on family size. What you needed was what you got. It wasn't Grace's psychologist job, but Leon's government position, managing City Center, that enabled their lifestyle which was more lavish than most.

"We've heard a little bit about you, but even that has been a stretch considering Braiden's passion for talking," Grace spoke sarcastically. "Tell me a little about yourself." Her hair was pulled back in a ponytail, and she wore a pair of old faded jeans complete with an oversized purple sweater.

"I'm almost eighteen, an only child, I love to dance and I have really high hopes of moving to Headquarters upon graduation."

"Krissa, if you ever want the inside scoop on Headquarters,

I'd be happy to give you the run down since I lived there many years before transferring here. It's a great place to be, lots of opportunities, and I keep telling Braiden to give it a chance."

Looking over at Leon who also had on a pair of blue jeans with a blue sweatshirt that had our government's symbol screen-printed across the chest, I felt very comfortable around these people. "Thank you. I'd love to hear all about it."

"Maybe another time." Braiden encouraged our departure.

I wasn't quite ready to leave given I was enjoying spending time with his parents.

"Well, it was very nice to meet you both, but I guess we'll get going."

"It was nice to meet you as well," his mom replied. "Hopefully we'll see you again soon."

"I hope so," I said as we headed toward the garage. "Goodnight." I waved good-bye and walked out the door.

"I told you they'd love you," Braiden said as I started my car.

"Yeah, I think that went well. Your parents are really nice."

"They're all right," he said. He looked over at me with that devilish grin, stirring up feelings in the depths of my stomach. It wasn't an inviting, warm smile but more of a dangerous, sly smirk that left me feeling uncertain, but wanting more.

"So, will they have a chance to get to know me better?" I asked, hoping to hear the answer I wanted.

"We'll see."

****

"Are you sure your parents don't mind us being here?" We finished dinner not long ago and were back at my house given my parents were out for the evening.

"No, they won't mind. They trust me," I said as we made our way into the living room.

"Oh, is that so? Well, no one ever said anything about trusting me, now, did they?" He wrapped his arms around me with a powerful grace that found me quickly on the couch while kissing my neck and moving his hands along my body. The longer he lay on top of me, the harder it was to resist him. He kissed me hard, and I couldn't stop the sensation running through my body. I pushed him off and stood up. He was stunned, not sure as to why I stopped him.

I grabbed his hand and led him through the hallway toward my bedroom. We strolled into my room, a small, typical girl room with an overstuffed closet. I turned on my music player and led Braiden toward my bed; happy there wasn't another option for seating. Sitting down on the satin sheets, I began to slowly undress. I pulled my long white V-neck sweater over my head, revealing a white lace push up bra, along with our Capital's symbol located right under my left collarbone. Upon birth, every infant born in our country was lasered with the prestigious emblem of our Headquarters.

He traced his fingers along the mark, "Do you ever wish you could remove this?"

Surprised by the question, I hesitated. I'd never given it much thought, especially because I had no intention of defying our government. "I've never thought about it. It's part of who I am."

"Do you ever think there might be a way around it?"

"I don't know, I've never thought about it."

"I just feel like they've branded us. Like we are a piece of property and they own us."

I fell silent, not sure how to respond to that.

"Forget I even asked, sometimes my brain just wonders."

"I understand." I said, even though I didn't.

Braiden seemed to put our conversation in the back of his mind and picked up where we left off. "Are you sure you want to do this?" Braiden asked hesitantly.

"I'm sure." I lay back on my bed, unbuttoned my jeans and wiggled out of them. I was sure that I felt something real with him, sure I wanted to be with him, and quite sure I was falling in love with him.

He slowly unbuttoned his shirt to reveal his amazing body and slid next to me. He kissed my shoulder and collarbone kissing a path to the bottom of my chin and eventually my mouth. He pulled himself onto me carefully, bracing with an arm above my head. His other hand outlined the curves of my body, while his tongue traced my lips. He smoothly removed my bra, exposing my breast, then, used both hands to remove the last piece of my clothing. While staring at my naked body, he stripped himself of his remaining clothes and brought his perfect body down onto mine, touching his bare skin against mine.

"I think I'm falling in love with you," I blurted out, without thinking.

"I know," he whispered in my ear with a grin spread across his beautiful face. Only this time his smile had no affect on me, I was too distracted by his words. I felt rejected. While my words didn't break his stride, he broke my concentration. I tried to remain in sync with him, but I felt disconnected. We were out of rhythm, in more ways than one.

Five

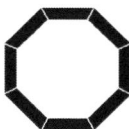

I was more attached to Braiden emotionally, and I accepted that. It was okay that he didn't love me yet. Fairly certain he would one day—at least that was my hope—I would continue to love him, longing for him to catch up.

December twelfth finally rolled around, it was my birthday. I wasn't expecting anything spectacular. After all, I was dating someone who seemed to be emotionally detached. When I found a beautiful bouquet of flowers staring me in the face when I opened my locker that day, I was euphoric. Maybe he *was* starting to change.

"Those flowers were amazing! Thank you so much!" I told him as we made our way through the busy hall to our first class.

"What flowers?" he responded with that killer smile.

"Shut up! You know what I'm talking about."

"Who gave you flowers? Am I going to have to kick someone's ass?"

"All you need to say is 'You're welcome, Krissa.' Well, that and you could throw in a happy birthday."

"You're welcome." He gave a quick peck to my forehead and whispered in my ear, "Happy Birthday. I've got to run, class starts in five minutes. I'll see you at lunch." He rushed off down the hallway, making his way around the other students.

While I was relishing in all the efforts Braiden made, Joy approached me.

"Hey Krissa! Happy birthday!"

"Hey Joy. Thanks."

"Wow, beautiful flowers. Braiden?" she asked hesitantly.

"Of course." I replied, laughing off her hesitation.

"So, did you do it?"

"Do what?"

"Make the appointment for your laser marking?"

"Oh, that. I'm actually going to wait."

"What? Why? You've been dying to get one, what changed?"

Since my early teens, I'd known I wanted another laser marking. I like that I could be unique and add creativity to my body, and looked forward to the day I was able to get one. That was until Braiden expressed his extreme dislike of them. It wasn't that Braiden told me I couldn't get one, more like he would be turned off at the sight of the marking on my skin. "Nothing, really. Braiden and I were talking about it and I just decided I'm not ready. I don't even know what I want. How can I have something permanently placed on my body, if I'm not sure about it?" I didn't look her in the eyes, instead keeping my focus elsewhere, like her cute wedge, knee-high boots and body-hugging blue sweater. I knew if I met her eyes, they'd burn through my façade and see the lies I was trying so hard to believe.

"I guess," she responded, not really sounding as if she bought my excuse. "Well, I've got to run. I just wanted to wish you a happy birthday."

"I'll see you around."

I knew she didn't agree with my decisions, but it was the fact that she seemed so disappointed in me that was bothersome. I was sure the time would come where I'd get another marking, I just wasn't ready to make that decision yet.

****

I wasn't expecting anything else for my birthday, but there was more to come. When we entered Braiden's house later that afternoon, he sat me on the couch and told me to close my eyes.

"Keep your eyes closed Krissa, no peeking!"

"I'm not," I exclaimed, both hands covering my closed eyes.

"Okay, open your eyes," he sat next to me. "Happy birthday." He placed a basket on my lap.

"You didn't have to do this, you've already done enough," I said, ripping away the tissue paper.

"Well, I know it's all of your favorites."

He was right. I went through the basket full of all the things I loved. I found my favorite perfume, a wonderfully scented candle, my favorite lip-gloss, and a picture of the two of us taken from the homecoming dance. "You did too much."

"Does that mean you like it?"

"Like it? I love it. I love you," I said quietly in a hushed voice, almost embarrassed to hear myself say it out loud. I wasn't expecting him to say it in return, but today was my day and I wanted him to know how I felt, wanted him to know that he was loved. "You don't need to say anything." And he didn't. Braiden kissed me on my forehead and laid me down on the couch. At least it was better than *I know*.

The following weekend was our senior mid-year Holiday dance, which Braiden and I planned on attending. He arrived at my house at 6:30 looking his best. It was baffling how he still made me nervous. He looked at me with a smile, "Wow, Krissa, you're breathtaking."

My hair was swept off my face and pinned in neat curls and I was almost at his eye level with my heels on. My rhinestone-studded dress hugged my body in the right places.

"Thank you, you look fantastic as well." I walked across the living room and planted a kiss on his lips. He kissed me, reluctantly, hearing my parents in the kitchen.

"Are you ready for the paparazzi?" I asked jokingly.

"I'm ready for my close up," he led me into the kitchen.

"Hello, Braiden," my mom said as we walked in. "It's nice to see you again."

"Hi, Faith."

"Hello, Sir," Braiden said to my dad as he reached out his hand.

"You guys ready for pictures?" My dad asked. My dad was

slightly obsessive compulsive with picture taking, which I didn't mind, but Braiden did. After several rounds of photos, I was beginning to sense Braiden's annoyance, so I called it quits and headed for the door.

"Love you guys. I'll call you later," I called back.

"Have fun tonight, be safe," my mom yelled to us as we got into my car. My mom, the worrier, would've really been worried had she known our real plans for the evening. I was eighteen; therefore, I could legally rent a hotel room. I acquired a room for all of my friends to have a place to hang out before the dance. The hospitality business was pretty much non-existent due to the lack of travelers. Every unit had two hotels, an expensive lavish one, and the low-end budget hotel which suited perfectly for our needs.

"Come on, girls, picture time!" I yelled to Hope, Honor, Joy, and Charity. We lined up against the wall and made our dates snap tons of pictures. We all looked gorgeous and were ready to party.

"Wait, one more," Joy said. She was stunning in her long, emerald gown. Although she was the shortest and the most petite, she stood out in a crowd.

Her date, Gabriel, was more than happy to take pictures with her. Gabriel and Joy had just started dating, but they were pretty serious. Gabriel had a small frame but stood tall. His dark hair was neatly gelled in place, and with glasses, he looked exceptionally studious. I had no doubt they'd eventually be paired.

"Are you doing okay?" I turned my attention to Charity who was standing next to me.

"Yes, today's been good." She knew I was referring to her relationship.

"I'm glad." I put my arm around her and we smiled for another picture.

Charity was also a beauty, her Italian background attributing to her looks. Her dark pin-straight hair framed her flawless, slightly freckled face and gorgeous deep blue eyes. Her long halter dress showed off her tall, slender figure.

Her date for the evening was her on-again off-again boyfriend, Victor. They loved each other one day but the next, they were cursing each other out. Tonight they seemed to be in love, but then again, it was early. For someone as beautiful as Charity, Victor's fault was making her feel inadequate.

I glanced towards Victor as he popped the cap off another beer. Victor was the rebel of the group, having several piercings and laser markings. He was good looking with dirty blonde hair that grew just past his ears. He didn't play sports and didn't have as many common interests as the rest of us, but he fit in pretty well. Everyone liked him just fine with the exception of that no one liked the way he treated Charity.

After pictures, everyone began to indulge in a few drinks. Considering the legal drinking age was eighteen, most of us weren't breaking the law. Those under age didn't feel too bad considering they weren't too far off from being legal. Even though

I'd just turned eighteen, I opted to be the designated driver. I took a seat next to Hope and Noble who also decided to stay sober.

"I'm so glad you guys came tonight."

Hope wore a short, black spaghetti strap dress covered with silver sparkles. Her long, perfect blonde hair flowed down to the middle of her back. Noble looked handsome as well wearing a black ensemble with a silver tie, complimenting his date.

"I know it's not really your scene, Noble, but I'm happy you're here." Noble had dreams of becoming an enforcer and wouldn't take part in anything that would jeopardize his future goals.

"It's all right, as long as Hope is having a good time."

She leaned forward and gave Noble a kiss. "How about you, Krissa? Are you enjoying yourself? You did a great job getting everyone together."

"Thanks, I'm enjoying it. I'm glad everyone is having fun."

Before long the guys were acting crazy and the girls were getting giggly. Gabriel, Emery, Victor and Braiden were engaged in a serious game of power hour while the girls gossiped and sipped on their beverages. After an hour or so, most of us piled into Gabriel's parents' car, having a large family worked to our advantage. I was pumped about getting the chance to drive such a large vehicle.

"Are we all set?" I asked as I began to pull out of the hotel parking lot.

"We're all set," Honor yelled from the backseat. She leaned over her seat into the trunk area and planted a kiss on Emery. Her girl-next-door look attracted all sorts of attention, especially from her date. They started dating only a month ago but seemed to be totally into each other. I liked Emery for the most part, but because he was a year younger than Honor, it made me nervous. I already felt like guys were four steps behind girls on the maturity scale. Would he be everything that she wanted and needed in a pairing?

I glanced in my rearview mirror and noticed Hope and Noble were holding hands, she was nestled into his arms. They never had a problem showing affection toward each other. Actually, it was a little sickening at times because I was accustomed not to show any affection. Deep down I was jealous. I was constantly wondering if Braiden was embarrassed. Why didn't Braiden show affection to me in public? Was he embarrassed because everyone would know he cared for someone or embarrassed because it was me? Due to our social status, I assumed he would've wanted to show that we were dating. I wanted to be his arm candy and was proud to be with him. I didn't mind flashing our relationship, and it would've been a good look on his part. I know that may sound conceited, but in the high school world, popularity and social standing were a top priority. I could never grasp why Braiden was so unwilling to put us on display. He made me over-think everything, so I analyzed every aspect of us. What did I need to do differently?

Six

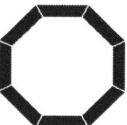

The dance came and went, and luckily for me, Chance had come down with the stomach bug and wasn't able to attend. Every opportunity he had Chance continued to tell me how much he missed me, and it made me nervous that he might tell Braiden he wanted me back. Or that he might even try and come between us. I knew Chance was good at manipulating the truth and I certainly didn't need Chance telling Braiden twisted lies.

On Saturday, my dad's family arrived at our house to celebrate Christmas. My dad, mom and I always traveled to my mother's family's unit for the actual holiday, so every year we celebrated with my dad's side before we left. As the four families poured into our house, my dad greeted everyone and took their coats. Braiden and I stood in the living room as my family came in saying hellos, and I excitedly introducing everyone to him.

"Felicity, I haven't seen you in forever! You look great." I said, because she always did. She was a short, petite girl with blonde, bouncy, shoulder length hair and fair, freckled porcelain skin. "Where is Gregory?"

"He stayed at Headquarters. He had to work, so he's going to spend the holiday with his family. You look great too. How's school going? Have you decided where you want to go yet?"

"I have an idea, but nothing concrete. Do you love Headquarters?" It was her number one choice four years ago upon graduation.

"Yes, I love it. You should visit sometime."

"I'd like that. Are you content with your choice?"

"Yes, I'm happy there."

"This is my boyfriend, Braiden." I said, not forgetting my manners as I nudged him forward.

"Hey," Braiden said to Felicity.

"It's nice to meet you. So, how'd you guys meet?"

"We go to school together," I responded.

"Oh nice," Felicity said. "Do you have any plans for next year, Braiden?"

"Not really. I think I'd like to stay in our unit." I don't think anyone noticed the change in his demeanor as he answered, but I saw the shift.

"Oh," Felicity said, thrown a little off-guard by the lack of response. "Well good luck picking when the time comes." Turning to me she said, "I'm going to go say hi to everyone, we'll chat again later."

"Okay. Catch you later."

Once the entire family was settled in, our small house felt claustrophobic. It was loud and chaotic but everyone seemed to have a good time. Considering we weren't the most social family, we ate, opened presents, and soon after, everyone headed home.

By nine o'clock our house was empty. My mom was standing over the sink finishing cleaning the kitchen while my dad picked up all the wrapping paper and trash in the living room. The timing couldn't have been better because Braiden and I had plans to go the movies.

"Can we help you with anything else, Mom?" I asked as I made my way into the kitchen.

"No, everything is pretty much taken care of. You kids can head on out. Thank you for all of your help."

"No problem. The movie is at 9:30, we should be back around 11:30."

As we drove to the only movie theater in town, I couldn't hold back my happiness.

"Did you have a good time tonight? I know my family can be a little crazy."

"Yes, I did. I don't usually do the whole family thing, you know."

"I know, that's why I'm so grateful you came. It really meant a lot to me. What did you think of my cousin's kids?" I asked, referring to her mini-terrors, ages one and three.

"I'm not really a kid person so, I'm glad they aren't mine. They're wild," Braiden said.

"What? The constant fighting and screaming didn't win you over?"

"No, not so much," Braiden said, laughing.

I tried to keep it light but the underlying topic of children was so heavy. It consistently weighed heavy on my mind.

We pulled into the parking lot and parked as close to the cinemas as possible. It was the dead of winter, meaning every time you walked outside, your body almost went into a state of shock. We ran as fast as our stiff bodies would allow until we reached the entrance. We entered the double doors to an empty corridor. Braiden and I didn't expect the movies to be busy because this time of year most people were either throwing holiday parties or were out of town to be with their families during the holidays. I'm visiting family for a whole week starting tomorrow, and it's going to be hard being apart.

****

"So what did you think of the movie?" I asked Braiden later as we exited the theater and got into my car.

"I thought it was pretty good if not predictable. Another film put out by our government, lacking creativity," he said, leaning back, finally satisfied with a song choice.

"True," I'd never thought of movies that way.

We discussed the movie the rest of our short drive home.

"Are you ready for your gifts?" I asked, a shy smirk on my face.

"Gifts, as in plural? How many did you get me? You better not have spent a lot of money," Braiden said, his serious tone.

"I didn't spend a lot, don't worry," I explained as I unlocked my front door. "You'll like all of it; that's all that matters."

We went to my bedroom in anticipation. "We've got to be quiet, my parents are already asleep. I don't want to wake them."

"I think I can handle it," he said as he kissed my forehead, giving me tingles.

"Is it alright if I give you your stuff first?" I asked him. He nodded. "Sit down," I instructed him. As Braiden sat, I reached to the back of my closet and pulled out the wrapped gifts. "Open this one first." I handed him a rectangular box.

"Okay", he took the wrapped box from me. Inside was a pair of grey sweatpants with stripes down the side. I admit this gift was a little selfish on my part, but I was tired of looking at him in the same old blue sweatpants. They were well received considering he'd already changed into them. The next gift I handed him was a smaller box wrapped in gold.

"Oh, a new bottle of cologne, thank you. I really needed this. I'm almost out, and it's my favorite."

"I know," I replied. He wore his signature scent every day; it was burned into my senses. "I saw that you were almost out when we were at your house the other day."

"Of course. Thank you."

"Okay, last one." I handed him a smaller wrapped box as I grinned barely able to hold back my excitement. Inside the box was a tri-fold black leather wallet he had mentioned he wanted a while back.

"This is the exact one I wanted," he said standing up to give me a hug.

He had very specific taste. "I know." I felt really proud of myself for making him happy, because that was all my life seemed to be about lately. If he was happy, so was I.

"Your turn." He went to the top drawer of my vanity and pulled out a small box wrapped in red and green Christmas paper.

"When did you hide that there?" I asked surprised. Not much got past me.

"Tonight, while you were talking with your family. I snuck in here to hide it from you."

"Tricky." I reached out my hand. Braiden placed the box in my hand, and as quickly as I could, I ripped off the wrapping. Inside was a black, velvet box. I looked at Braiden, making sure this was the right gift.

"Go ahead, what are you waiting for?"

I opened the box and found the necklace I'd shown him a couple of weeks back. To be honest, I didn't think he was even paying attention when we were window-shopping downtown after dinner that night. The necklace was on display in one of the local jewelers, and I loved it. It was a thin, white gold chain that supported a unique heart locket. It was perfect.

"Open it," Braiden said. I expected to see a picture of him, or of both of us, but instead it was a date. *October 15th* was written in beautiful script right inside of the heart. I looked at the inscription stunned, because I knew what the date was; I just never imagined Braiden did.

"It's the day we *officially* became us," Braiden said, using air quotes around the word officially.

"I know," I gasped.

How could I not? October fifteenth had been one of the best nights of my life. My parents had gone out with some friends as they usually did on the weekends, ans I decided to have a few friends over, which my parents were fine with. Braiden and I ended up on the couch together and that's when it happened. It was the first time I put my lips to his. The intensity between us was undeniable and I never wanted my lips to experience anyone else's.

"You just looked confused," Braiden said bringing me out of the memory of our first kiss.

"No, I'm just surprised you remembered." My gift was perfect. I threw my arms around him and gave him countless kisses. "Remember we have to be quiet." I said innocently.

"I'll try my best, but I'm not guaranteeing anything," he said slyly pulling me down on the bed.

Being with Braiden was like nothing I'd ever come across. Regardless of how much I had of him, I wanted more. He was intriguing, mysterious and simply exquisite. He was all I'd ever wanted but never knew I was in such need. There was something different about that night. Maybe it was the holiday spirit or maybe I was so taken back by his thoughtful gift, I don't know. But I felt different. Whatever it was, something had changed within me.

Seven

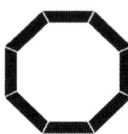

The time spent with my family passed almost too quickly; I always enjoyed visiting the Educators unit. They lived similar to us but were a bit more high tech. I'd always felt as if I gained knowledge when we were there, given everywhere I turned I was bombarded with information. The library, schools, and museums were beautiful institutions that flooded a stream of information into my brain. While I enjoyed my time with family, I was eager to be back in the presence of Braiden.

It wasn't until New Year's Eve that I got to see him. Our town always hosted *First Night* to celebrate the New Year, meaning all sorts of activities took place in downtown. Our dance team had been asked to perform, and we happily obliged.

"Hey girl," Honor said as I picked her up on our way to City Center.

"Hey! How was your Christmas? Did Emery like his gift?"

"It was nice, and yes, he loved the new sneakers."

"Good, what did he get you?"

"He got me some music and this bracelet," she said as her

arm stretched out showing off the gold bangle.

"It's gorgeous!"

"I know! His mom helped him pick it out," she said.

"Who cares, as long as you like it? He did a good job." It was her, simple yet classy.

"By any chance did Braiden give you that necklace you're wearing?" Honor asked.

"Yes, and it gets better."

"What do you mean?" I leaned towards her and told her to open the locket. "What's that date?"

"The day we became *official*," I explained.

"I can't believe he did that, it's so unlike him." By now all of my friends had observed his unaffectionate ways.

"Tell me about it; it took me off guard too! Emery's coming tonight, right?"

"Yeah. Do you and Braiden want to grab some food afterwards?" she asked.

"Sure, we're not really doing anything," I answered.

"Okay, cool. We'll see where the boys want to go."

"All right."

We pulled into the parking lot next to the City Center building in the heart of downtown. The two-story brick building housed the Regulators' offices—all city information and records—and the large auditorium was used mostly for meetings. It also housed a few holding cells for the rare occurrence's when civilians acted out, which I'd never seen.

"Look at all the people," Honor said as we walked around the chairs.

"We're so popular!" I joked while doing my best valley girl imitation.

Hope was there to support our team with Noble and next to them sat Braiden and Emery. "I missed you," I whispered in Braiden's ear.

"I know you did, I missed you too," Braiden responded.

"You did?" I asked, surprised by his response.

"Yes, I did."

I squeezed him a little tighter and told him I had to go get ready for the show. "Come on Honor, let's go." I led her to the small bathroom outside the auditorium entrance.

"See you guys out there."

"Break a leg," Emery called out to us.

It seemed like everyone we knew was there. While it wasn't our greatest performance, it was fun.

"Well that was interesting," my dad said to me after the show was over. "You guys were practically on top of one another! You need a bigger space."

"I know. I think one of the girls actually got kicked in the head during the fan kicks."

"I wouldn't say it was my favorite show, but at least you had fun," Mom said.

"We did our best. It was hard to keep on beat considering the music kept skipping. I'm going to go grab some food with Braiden,

Honor and Emery, and then I think Braiden and I are going to watch the countdown from home."

"Okay," Mom said. "You guys have fun. We're going to stay down here for the fireworks, and we'll be home after that."

I gave my parents a hug and hustled to catch up to Braiden.

"Our show was ridiculous. I hope someone got that on camera, we were awful," I said, slipping my arm around his waist. He stood starring down a long dark hallway.

"What do you think is down there?" he asked suspiciously.

"I don't know, why?"

"Do you think it's a way to the cells?"

"I don't know, and I don't care. Come on, Honor and Emery are waiting." He was scaring me, standing there frozen with curiosity. I wasn't sure what was running through his mind and why he cared so much, but I didn't want anything to do with it. I tugged on his arm, encouraging our departure, but he ignored me.

"Let's find out." He started down the corridor toward the large metal door.

"No, Braiden, don't," I called, but before I could convince him, his hand was on the door handle, and he disappeared behind it.

My heart was racing. We both knew we weren't allowed in that part of the building and while I didn't want to get in trouble, I was more worried about him. I ran after him hoping to stop his foolishness. "Braiden?" I whispered as I closed the door behind me. My eyes were adjusting to the dim lighting when I realized I was standing before a winding staircase leading down to a place I didn't want to know about.

"I'm down here."

"Well, come back up here," I pleaded.

"Come here, check this out." His enthusiasm was making even me more nervous.

"No, we're going to get in trouble, please come back."

I took his silence for a no, so I carefully made my way down the stairs, one hand on the railing the other sliding along the cold concrete wall.

"Look at this." He stood in front of a large, steel door with a sign that clearly stated *Do Not Enter-Enforcements Only*. "I wish I had the code," he was looking at an electronic box with a screen and pin pad on the wall to the right of the door.

"Well, you don't, so let's go."

"Krissa, do you really think people are in those cells?"

"No, I don't."

He went to argue but before he could get the words out, we could hear the latch on the other side of the door being unlocked. "Quick, come on." He grabbed my hand, and we raced up the stairs.

"Hey! Who are you?" We heard the large, booming voice behind us as we sprinted through the top floor door.

I didn't stop running until we reached my car. "Hurry, get in. Do you think they knew it was us? I'm scared. I don't want to get in trouble."

"Don't worry, Krissa, they'll never know. Relax."

I pulled out of the parking lot, still out of breath, my heart in my throat and my hands damp with sweat. "Why would you do that?"

"I was curious. Go to Nina's." He pointed to the right, directing me. "Emery just sent me a message to meet them there."

How was he so calm? I was scared shitless. "That's it? Curious? We could have gotten into a lot of trouble."

"We're fine. Get over it. Nothing happened."

I wasn't sure what to say because he was right nothing happened, but something could have.

****

Nina's had the best pizza in town. However, I was on edge thinking Enforcements were roaming the streets looking for us. I needed a distraction.

"What are you guys doing after this?" I asked Honor and Emery as we sat in a booth near the back of the restaurant.

"We're going to my house to count down the New Year among other things," Emery said honestly.

"Emery! Shut up!" Honor slapped him on the arm then buried her face in her hands.

"What? We've got to bring in the New Year with style," he responded back.

"Okay, enough! No details needed please," I said.

After glaring at Emery for a minute, Honor turned to me. "What are your plans for the rest of the night?"

"Not much. Just going home to watch the Headquarters broadcast of the New Year countdown, nothing fancy," I lied. I had plenty in mind.

We chatted about nothing important as we ate our food.

"Well," Emery said after finishing his pizza, "I guess we're going to go ... we've got things to do," he playfully nudged my best friend.

"I'm going to kill you," Honor said to Emery. "Bye guys. Have a good New Year's," she yelled back to us as she chased Emery out of the restaurant.

"He's crazy," I said to Braiden.

"He was just stating what you were thinking."

"True," I said, as I felt my cheeks darken.

"Well, are you ready to go celebrate?"

"Yes, but first will you tell me what you were thinking back at City Center?"

"Drop it Krissa, seriously." He rose and made his way to the exit.

I didn't want to drop it. I was disturbed with the way he acted and the danger he put us in. I also knew if he didn't want to discuss it, he wouldn't.

The house was ours for several hours, so we were going to take advantage of it. Having no intention of watching the countdown, our world would still be the same at midnight as it was a minute before, we were more interested in one another. We steamed up the shower and made love several times. I loved every minute with him, and I figured, all our good outweighed our bad.

****

It was back to school on Monday, but more focus was on the upcoming dance than school. In the back of my mind I still had thoughts that we were going to be in trouble for our detour at the City Center, but after a few days, I guessed we were in the clear. Honor and I planned to go to the dance together hoping to play catch-up on our friendship. Feeling as if I neglected our relationship since Braiden walked into my life, I thought this dance would be the perfect opportunity to reconnect. Braiden agreed, taking advantage of a night with the boys.

"Hey," I said as she came into my bathroom. "You look great!" She had on tight fitting dark wash jeans and an adorable one-strap shirt.

"I love your outfit, too!"

I looked in the mirror over the single counter sink and decided I looked good enough. I had on lighter wash jeans and a shirt that cut low in the front. "I'm almost ready. I just need to put my hair up."

"We've got plenty of time."

I threw my hair up in a messy, cute ponytail with the front part side swept across my forehead. I did a three hundred and sixty degree turn in the mirror and decided I was good. "All right, I'm all set. Are you ready?"

"I'm ready. I'm driving, missy, because we both know you

can't in those sky-high shoes."

"Very true."

"Okay, Mom, we're leaving," I yelled.

"All right, you girls have fun and be safe."

I'd been so wrapped up in my relationship, I'd forgotten how much fun Honor and I had together. I needed better balance in my life. But as much as I wanted to divide myself equally between my boyfriend and my friends, I always managed to favor Braiden.

As we walked to Honor's, car bundled up in heavy coats trying very hard not to fall on my icy driveway, we strategized about the night's festivities. "Where do you think we should go?" She asked as we got into her car.

"What do you think about the park?" I asked cranking up her heat. "There's no way anyone would be there."

"Sounds good to me." She pulled out of my driveway. "I'm so glad we're doing this." She looked over at me. "I feel like we never get to spend any time together anymore."

"I know. Things have been so hectic lately. I've been so busy with dance, the holidays—"

"Braiden," she interrupted.

"I know, and I'm sorry. He does consume a lot of my time. I really will try harder to have more girl nights. I've missed you, too."

She accepted my words and believed I'd attempt to make more time for her. I wanted to believe it too, I just wasn't sure how to juggle everyone and keep them all happy. They were all a very important part of my life, but I felt that I needed to keep Braiden my top priority if I wanted him to remain in my life. After all, he was the only one who could give me what I really wanted.

We drove until we reached the park, hiding behind the playground. "Perfect," I said as I pulled out the vapor weed pipe. It was insane they banned marijuana, especially since the old world legalized it in every state. What happened to those days?

We'd made our way to the dance when our supply was gone, grabbing some food along the way. We walked into our school, slightly apprehensive, thinking maybe one of the teachers would notice we were high, but we had no problem. Walking toward the cafeteria, an enforcer stepped out of the shadows blocking our path.

"Miss Channing?"

"Yes?" I started sweating.

"May I have a word with you alone, please?"

Oh shit, he knew I was high. It was illegal to use drugs, no one ever really got into trouble for it, so why was I being singled out? "Am I in trouble?"

"Not yet."

Not yet? What did that mean? He looked so intimidating in his uniform. I followed him around the corner glancing back at Honor who looked both confused and worried for me. "I'll be right back, Honor, go find Emery and have fun." I sounded brave, but was a ball of nerves as I followed Mr. Enforcer into the school's office.

"Let's go in here." He led me into Principal Maxx's office. "Have a seat." He pointed to the poorly upholstered chair that sat across from the principal's desk.

I took a seat, and watched him pull out his communicator from his utility belt.

"This, Miss Channing, is a surveillance video that was recorded at City Center the night of New Year's Eve."

"Okay." Swallowing the large lump that was forming in my throat, I was thinking I was in here for being high; I wasn't expecting this. My brain was too clouded for this conversation.

He pressed play. "This is you, correct?"

I watched myself running behind Braiden up the stairs, quickly followed by an enforcer. "Yes, sir. That's me." I didn't meet his cold stare.

"Care to elaborate as to what you were doing?"

Think Krissa! "Um," I shifted uncomfortably in my seat, "I wasn't paying attention when I exited and wound up there. I, uh, got lost."

"Lost?"

"Yes. I'm very sorry for the confusion." I looked up at him, hoping he would buy my story. He was younger than I anticipated, maybe a few years older than myself, and pretty attractive. He looked strong and rugged in the all black government attire, and the large gun tucked into his belt certainly added to the intimidation. "So am I in trouble?"

He ignored my question. "Who was with you?"

I looked at the screen again. Braiden's face was never exposed. He wore a black hat and kept his head down the entire time the camera was on us. "Um," I hesitated.

"Miss Channing, it's a simple question."

I knew the answer, but I didn't want to get Braiden in trouble. If I lied would they be able to figure it out? "It's a good friend of mine."

"You didn't answer my question."

"It wasn't his fault, he came to find me."

"Name."

"Braiden. Braiden Connor."

"Thank you. You say he came to find you?"

"Yes." All I saw was the part where we were running up the stairs; I was praying that was all the footage they had.

"Because you got lost?"

"Yes, sir." I sounded weak.

"Okay, thank you for your time, Miss Channing."

"That's all?" I was surprised he was dismissing me.

"Is there more you'd like to share?"

"No, sir," I responded quickly. "So, I'm not in trouble?"

"According to your story, there's no reason to be."

"Right, okay. And Braiden? Will you talk to him?"

"No, ma'am, I just needed to hear what took place. Thank you for your time. You may go now."

"Thank you." I hopped up quickly and headed for the door.

"Miss Channing, we'll be watching. You're on our radar now."

What did that mean? I raced out of the office as quickly as I could. What was I supposed to do now? Tell Braiden? I didn't want to upset him, but I was in this position because of him! I'd piqued the interest of the Enforcers, and not in a good way. Was that going to hurt my chances of going to Headquarters? I wanted to do right by me, but I also wanted to do right by Braiden.

I walked into the cafeteria, making my way around bodies in motion in search of Braiden and saw him standing against the wall looking a little irritated.

"Hey." I hugged him, relieved to be in his arms.

He peeled me off of him. "Where have you been? What took you so long to get here?" he asked in an accusing tone. He sounded angry, and looked furious. "And what the hell are you wearing? Do you think you could have worn a shirt that cut a little lower? Whose attention are you trying to attract, Krissa?"

I was stunned by his questions, and he didn't even give me a chance to explain myself. I didn't understand where any of this was coming from.

"Why did Honor get here before you did?" he said, still berating me with questions.

"I'm not that late. I got hung up on my way in here." I wasn't ready describe my conversation with the Enforcer. I protectively wrapped my arms around my body, trying to cover myself. "And what's wrong with my shirt? You've seen it before and never said anything." I tried to diffuse the situation.

"I've been waiting for you. As for the shirt, I just don't like it."

"I'm sorry. I didn't think we were that late." I pulled him away from the crowd afraid we were causing a scene.

"Yeah, but you said you'd be here at nine o'clock."

"It's only 9:30." I pointed to the clock on the far wall.

"Well maybe you would've been on time if you weren't so busy getting high."

I pulled myself closer to him, looking around making sure no one was noticing our argument. "Oh please, Braiden. Spare me the double standard. I can only imagine what you and Chance did before coming here, so don't give me that shit. Don't throw stones when you live in a very breakable house. I'm sorry I upset you by being late, but let's just try to have some fun, okay?" I wanted to be strong and tried to sound as if I was, but inside, I felt a little weak.

"Okay," he finally said, reluctantly.

We made our way back into the crowd, and Honor's eyes caught mine.

"Everything okay?" she mouthed to me. I shook my head yes and smiled, but nothing felt fine. I was on the government's radar and had managed to piss off Braiden.

Fortunately, the rest of the evening was uneventful. I danced with my girlfriends to our favorite songs, but something was still off between Braiden and me. Maybe he wasn't the best choice. I still had time before preliminary pairing, so maybe I should consider running while I had the chance. Maybe I should stick to my original plan of moving to Headquarters and find my pair there. I loved him, yes, but was his happiness worth the expense of my own?

Eight

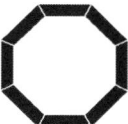

Enforcements didn't believe in the prevention of pregnancy, so birth control was hard to come by. Braiden and I neglected to use protection a few times, and I was nervous about missing my period.

When I started cramping and went to the bathroom during dance class, a huge wave of relief swept over me. I wasn't sure if this was because I didn't want to be pregnant, or because my future with Braiden was so uncertain. I don't know why I'd been so worried; we'd been irresponsible on several occasions and nothing ever came about it. I was ecstatic to share the good news with Braiden bearing in mind I already alarmed him that I was nervous about getting my monthly visit. As soon as I could, I left dance and drove straight to Braiden's basketball game to tell him the good news.

As I paced up and down the hall waiting for Braiden, Chance exited the locker room. "Hey Kris," Chance said, surprised to see me standing out there.

"Hey, Chance. Can you do me a favor and run in there," I

pointed to the boy's locker room, "and ask Braiden to come out here, please."

"Nice to see you, too, Krissa." His sarcasm wasn't lost on me.

"Please, Chance," I persisted.

"Fine." As he walked away from me, I heard him mutter, "This is such bullshit." Not concerning myself with his feelings, I just wanted to see Braiden.

"What's going on? What's wrong?" he asked, looking around the empty hall.

"Actually, everything is perfect."

"So what do you need?"

I flung my arms around him. "I got it!"

"Got what?" he asked confused.

"My period."

"Are you serious? Thank God. You had me worried."

"I had myself worried! Okay, I've got to get back to dance, have a good game. I'll see you tomorrow. Have fun tonight with your friends."

"I'll call you later when I get home. Thanks for bringing me good news."

"You're more than welcome. I'll talk to you later. Bye!"

It was good news, and I was happy to share it. I desperately wanted things to work with Braiden, but we were on such different paths. I didn't want to be forced into anything. I wanted to be paired with someone who loved me and shared the same goals and wasn't sure yet if that was possible with him. I was optimistic but realistic. Unbeknownst to Braiden, I had given our relationship an expiration date which consisted of only a few more months. I was hoping it would lead to a path of pairing, but if it wasn't, then I felt my only other choice was to walk away.

****

The following day, my world began to shatter. I never got my full period. It was only spotting, a common symptom of pregnancy. Braiden called when he returned home last night, but I wasn't in the mood to talk. I was cold and short with him, lost in my own thoughts. I had no idea what was going on with my body, and I was confused. If this relationship were with someone who loved me and wanted to pair, this pregnancy would be no big deal. Sure, it was a bit earlier than I'd planned, but eventually it would've happened. To be pregnant with Braiden's child was a completely different story.

I tried to get the words right while driving to Braiden's house, but nothing seemed to sound right.

"Hello Krissa," Grace said as she opened the door. "It's nice to see you again."

"Hi, it's nice to see you also. How have you been?" It was difficult for me to stand in front of her and put on a brave face, knowing the news I would be sharing with her son in a few minutes.

"Good, glad the hectic holidays are over."

"I bet," I replied.

"Braiden's in his room, you can go up."

"Thanks."

I walked up the staircase, praying I was dreaming and knowing a nightmare was now my reality.

"Hey, how are you?" I asked walking into Braiden's room. I tried to sound as normal as possible, but I couldn't stop the swarm of thoughts overtaking my brain.

"Tired. We got home late last night," Braiden said, sitting at the edge of his bed finishing his video game.

"I'm sorry I was short on the phone last night." I stood next to his bed, not making myself comfortable.

"Are you all right? You aren't acting like yourself."

"We need to talk."

"About what?" he asked, moving over to make room.

"This isn't easy for me to tell you." I ignored his offer and paced in front of him. "I've thought about all of the ways to say it, but nothing sounds right. Yesterday when I told you I'd started my period, I really thought I had. But now, I don't think I have."

"Wait, what? I'm not sure I'm following. What does that mean?"

"I think I'm pregnant. God, I can't believe I'm saying this." I was ashamed to finally hear myself say the words out loud.

"Are you fucking kidding me?" Braiden said jumping up with his hands clutched to his head, pacing back and forth.

"No! I'm not Braiden. I'm freaking out as well!" His response certainly wasn't helping the matter. He looked so mad, I instantly felt like he was blaming me. "What are we going to do?" I wanted to emphasize the *we* part, but I refrained from doing so.

"I ... I don't know," he said, while calming his voice. "Have you actually taken a test?"

"No." I hadn't had time to wrap my head around that.

"Okay. Well let's not freak out until anything is confirmed. Tomorrow after school we'll go to Healthcare and find out for sure."

"Okay." I couldn't help but notice his demeanor. I had a lot to deal with, but his cold attitude didn't help.

I didn't stay much longer after our conversation and was really at a loss for words. I thought about stopping at Healthcare on the way home to get tested, but I thought we should do it together.

I was a nervous wreck throughout the entire day, and while my friends noticed something was wrong, they didn't seem to push the issue when I told them, "I'm just not feeling well."

I met Braiden after my last class, eager to get going. "Hey, are you ready?"

"Listen, I can't go with you. The guys need me to go with them because Owen has some big secret he needs to tell us."

"Are you serious?" I asked infuriated.

"If I don't go they'll freak out and quiz me as to why I wasn't there." He moved closer to me, talking in a whisper.

"Who cares, make something up!" I wasn't trying to lower my tone. I was too angry to care if anyone saw us fighting.

"I care. I don't want them to be suspicious."

"You're unbelievable! I can't believe you're choosing to hear some secret over *this*," I said, pointing to my stomach.

"Just trust me on this," he said as he grabbed my arm, not allowing me to point any longer. "Give me a half hour with them. Go home, relax, and I'll be there soon."

"Whatever." Not minding my tone, I ripped my arm from his grasp and stormed past him. *Relax*? Like it was that easy.

It was 3:45—an hour had passed—and still no Braiden. I couldn't comprehend how I wasn't a priority. I was tired of waiting, and didn't need him. Frustrated, I left my house and made my way to Healthcare.

The glass exterior looked mirrored and towered over other buildings. The first section mainly consisted of different doctors' offices including a pediatric unit, general healthcare, elderly healthcare and a few outpatient offices. The back half was the hospital unit, for those having extended stays or emergencies.

I hurried through the double glass doors into a sterile looking hallway. Three large wooden doors were on each side of the long hallway, and I chose the first, the walk-in care clinic. "How may I help you?" A woman sitting behind the glass window asked. I studied her wrinkled face as I contemplated if I was doing the right thing.

"Hi, my name is Krissa." I looked around the waiting area, double-checking that we were alone. "I need to take a pregnancy test," I stated.

"Oh. Please fill out this paperwork." She passed me a

clipboard with several papers attached. "When you're finished, bring it back up. They'll call your name when they're ready for you." I could see the pity in her eyes when she glanced down at my ring finger and didn't see the lasered band marking.

"Thank you," I said to the woman, and she sat back down in her over-sized leather chair. I walked to the waiting area and took a seat in a chair that wasn't nearly as luxurious. I took a few minutes to offer my life story, and just as I completed the paperwork, my communicator alerted with a message.

It was Braiden. *Where are you?*

I was hesitant to respond because I was so angry, but he had a right to be here. *Healthcare, walk-in clinic.*

I'll be there soon.

Fantastic.

"Krissa?" the nurse said as she opened the large wood door, which led to the exam rooms.

"That's me," I replied, getting up from my chair.

"Come with me, please." The nurse was short and robust, wearing unflattering white scrubs. She held the door open for me, and I saw the look of concern on her face. I stood in front of the scanner that rattled off my height and weight then took the pregnancy device that required a urine sample. "It'll take two minutes to read once I push the button to run the scan. It will tell me the outcome, and then someone will be in to speak with you. Understand?"

"Yes." Holding the black device and following her instructions.

I prayed for a miracle. I held the flat rectangular unit in my hand, careful not to push any buttons, and willed it to read the way I wanted it to.

I took a seat in the exam room anxiously waiting to hear what deep down I already knew. I sat in the chair next to the counter because I didn't feel comfortable lying on the sterile, stiff bed. After all, I wasn't here for an exam or for a doctor to diagnose a problem. I already knew what the problem was, and no antibiotic or amount of rest would do me any good. I passed the time by looking at the posters hanging on the walls, concerning parenting and healthy habits, but nothing took my mind away from the issue at hand. A knock on the door was followed by a woman's voice.

"Krissa?"

"Yes."

"I'm Doctor Trinly. It's nice to meet you. I was told that your boyfriend is in the waiting room. Would you like him to join us?" I thought about it for a moment then decided to let him join.

"That would be okay," I answered.

She motioned for the nurse to fetch Braiden then sat down across from me. She sat a larger version of our communicators down on the table along with the pregnancy test device that was now lit up in green.

A few moments later Braiden pulled up a chair next to me, but I refused to look at him. The three of us sat in the small, box-like room ready to discuss what the pregnancy test revealed.

"Your pregnancy test came back positive, confirming you're

pregnant. Congratulations." I think she expected a response, but those words, even though I knew they were true, just left me numb.

"You're about four weeks pregnant." She pushed another button on the device and the date *September 22nd* appeared on the screen. "This is your anticipated due date. This isn't one hundred percent accurate, given all the factors that go along with pregnancy, but this is the best prediction as to when you'll deliver."

Braiden spoke up when he realized I wasn't going to. "Could you please explain our options?"

"Well, option number one," Doctor Trinly started, "is to keep the baby and raise him or her in a healthy, loving environment. Here are some pamphlets on where to begin, such as prenatal vitamins and what's needed for the baby's development." Dr. Trinly was extremely optimistic about this choice. The way she spoke about it made it seem as if that was the obvious option. "You'll be automatically paired."

"What are our other choices?" Braiden continued. Even though we needed to know what they were, something deep inside of me hated him for asking. That option wasn't perfect, but I considered it my only one.

"Other choices ... yes, sure." She apparently already thought we had made our choice to keep the baby.

She thought wrong.

She shifted uncomfortably in her chair. "Option two would be adoption, and if that's what you choose, we'd certainly help guide you through that process. There are many families that would love to take a baby into their home. You're not automatically paired as a result, however, it's highly likely Headquarters will pair you. And there's no guarantee you or your baby will stay in this unit. The last choice you have is abortion. We perform that procedure here, but as I'm sure you know, if that's what you choose, you'll be forced to remain un-paired and you'll be placed in the Sweepers unit. The Enforcements strongly discourage this option as they view it as an act of resistance. I'll report the pregnancy to Headquarters today, but you have five months to make your final decision. I'll be glad to help in any way I can. I know I've presented you with a lot of information. I'll give the two of you some privacy."

"Thank you," Braiden and I said simultaneously. Although we spoke in sync, I didn't feel as if we were on the same page at all.

"So on Friday, Pax had a party at his house and a bunch of people showed up except Tobin. Everyone got really drunk, and Owen ended up hooking up with Tobin's girlfriend. Now Owen is freaking out that Tobin's going to find out and kick his ass. He said he only did it because he was wasted, but he's real worried about what Tobin will do when he finds out."

"Are you kidding me right now?" I was so disgusted. I met his stare, hating what I saw.

"No, unfortunately I'm not. I can't believe he did that!"

"Really, Braiden?" I said a few tones louder. "That's what's occupying your thoughts right now? You really don't see a problem here?" I couldn't believe he was acting so foolish, so uncaring. He was more wrapped up in high school drama than real life problems. We were the last things on his mind.

"You're mad. I get it, but I'm here now."

"What are we going to do?" I asked, pulling my glare from him. I couldn't bear to look at him and see his distance. I was only able to deal with one problem at a time, so his lack of concern needed to go on the back burner. Braiden never wanted kids; I couldn't see my life without them. The timing was poor and I certainly didn't want to be pregnant now, but I was. I'd been contemplating what our future looked like, but it was like I was handed a map showing me the way. It wasn't ideal at that point in my life, but we could make it work, we *had* to make it work.

"I don't know, Krissa."

"I need to know how you feel. I can't read your mind. You have to talk to me."

"I don't know what to say!" He was acting out against me, like I was the one who caused all of this. "I never expected to have a conversation about having a child at seventeen." His tone was condescending, and it was starting to wear on me. I didn't want this either, but we had to face it. What were we supposed to do?

"I didn't ask for this either!" I fought back. "You think I wanted this? Do you think I planned this? Hell no! But I can't ignore it. I can't pretend everything's okay; I'm not a robot like *you*." Anger boiled within me.

We walked out of the office, barely acknowledging one another. I didn't want him to touch me or be near me. I went to open the driver's side door, but he blocked me.

"You aren't in the right state of mind to be driving, let me," he said as he reached for the keys.

I didn't have the energy to argue. "Here." I extended my arm and placed the keys in his hand. He shouldn't be driving, he only had his permit, but on this particular day, I didn't care. Honestly, I didn't care about anything. My world was falling apart.

I slumped down into the passenger seat and got lost in my thoughts as we made our way to Braiden's house.

"Krissa," Braiden said as he placed his hand on my shoulder once we were inside, "we'll get through this."

"I can't do this. I can't choose. How could I let this happen?" The tears continued to roll down my face while thoughts were swirling in my brain. If only birth control was more accessible, this would have never happened to us. As much as I wanted to blame Headquarters, the blame was still my own. The most logical solution for me was to keep the baby and to be paired, but a little voice in the back of my head told me that this wasn't what Braiden wanted. How could I give our baby away? And there was no way I was becoming a Sweeper.

As soon as we reached Braiden's I was ready to leave. "I have to go," I said in between sobs.

"Are you okay to drive?" he asked, sounding concerned.

"Yes, I need to get myself together before dance."

"You're going to go?" He seemed surprised.

"Yes. What am I supposed to do? Stay home and hide myself from the world?"

"That's not what I meant. You're a little fragile right now."

"I'll be okay," I lied. How could we be in the same situation yet see things so differently?

Nine

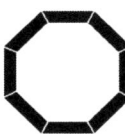

Telling my mom when I got home could've been the right decision, but I couldn't make myself say it. I went to dance as planned and when I returned home, I went to bed, not saying much to my parents. A knock at my door interrupted my thoughts.

"Krissa?" my mom called out cautiously as she opened my door.

"Yeah?" I replied as I lay in my bed with all of my lights off.

"Are you all right?" she asked, sounding concerned.

"I'm fine."

"You don't seem like yourself tonight. I just wanted to make sure everything was okay."

"Everything's fine, I'm just really tired."

"Well then, goodnight."

"Goodnight, Mom." She was standing outside of my bedroom door, contemplating. We had a great relationship and I felt guilty for lying, but I didn't know if she could handle the magnitude of my problem. I was scared as to how she'd react, embarrassment and shame. Her only daughter, pregnant. She did everything right. We had the talks, and I knew all about the birds and the bees, yet here I was. She had really high hopes for me, and my situation was sure to disturb the plan she had.

The following day went as normally as possible. I knew my friends were skeptical of my behavior, but I did my best to hide my emotions. During my most dreaded class, Joy approached me.

"Hey Krissa," Joy said as I emerged from the girls locker room, late again. "Way to be on time."

"I know, I know. Oh well." I knew my tardiness would go on un-noticed. It was only by four minutes, and Mrs. Sandars was way past retirement.

"Can I talk to you alone for a minute?" she asked as she grabbed my wrist and led me to the side of the bleachers.

"Sure." I didn't have much of a choice.

"I'm worried about you."

"You shouldn't be." I was defensive.

"You've become really distant and seem really upset and unhappy. Is there something going on between you and Braiden?" I half smiled and shook my head.

"Are you sure? You know you can talk to me if you need to."

"I know, Joy, thank you." As I started to walk away, she reached for my arm once again.

"I have to ask you this, is Braiden hurting you?" My facial reaction must have shown confusion because Joy felt the need to elaborate on the question. She continued, "I mean, does he put his hands on you?" she asked awkwardly.

"Oh my God, no! Why would you think that? He'd never!"

"All right," she said reluctantly. "You're just not the same to me. You look scared when you're around him. You never hold hands with him. You never show affection toward one another. You don't laugh anymore. It's like you're not even with it half the time. I'm not trying to hurt your feelings, but you seem lost. You used to be so exuberant and so full of life. I don't know why you're with him."

"Well I don't know about that, but we're fine, I swear. I have a lot going on with dance classes and I'm stressing about picking and pairing." I knew I was struggling to get those last words out, but I couldn't tell anyone what was really going on. It wasn't as simple as leaving him.

"I just wanted to make sure," Joy said. "Just know I'm always here for you."

"I know." I hugged her tightly, wishing I could tell her.

Internally, I scolded myself. I clearly wasn't putting up as good of a front as I'd thought. I'd been trying so hard to keep up appearances but I guess the pregnancy had gotten the best of me.

"It looks like someone else wants your attention now." She pointed across the gymnasium at Chance, who was making hand gestures, asking me to come his way.

"What the hell does he want?"

"Who knows," she said as she walked away to meet up with some of our other classmates.

"What's up, Chance?" I asked as I met him at the last badminton court.

"Not much. Want to play on my team?"

"Sure, whatever. So, how've you been?"

"Good, but I want to know how you are."

"Great, thanks. Why do you ask?"

"Well I've heard, uh …" He paused, looking around the room to see if we had anyone's attention.

"Go ahead, Chance, spit it out."

"I heard you and Braiden aren't doing so well," he said quietly, leaning into me.

"What?" My heart stopped beating for a brief moment as my mind tried to register what it heard. What did he mean?

"People have been talking. Saying the two of you have been arguing and not getting along."

I had to think of something quickly. "Oh, we had a little tiff the other day after school. We had plans, but he made other plans with you guys instead. It was the day you all went over to Owen's house. I was just upset, but I'm over it. No big deal." That was believable.

"You sure? You still seem upset."

"I'm not. We're fine, I promise." I stood still on the court, letting Chance do all the work.

"I guess I'm the unfortunate one then." He sucked in some air after a long volley.

"What do you mean?" I asked, confused.

"I was still hoping we had a chance."

"Chance," I said with a heavy sigh, "I can't do this."

"Do what?" he asked shrugging his shoulders.

"This!" I waved my hand in the space between our bodies. "How many times are we going to have this conversation? We had our chance, and it didn't work out. When you cheated on me, I told you you'd regret it and now you do. No matter what you hear about Braiden and me, we, as in you and I, will never be back together. I want to be with Braiden. I'm sorry." I took some of my anger and frustration out on him.

"I don't believe you, and I'm not giving up."

"You need to." I put my racket back in the bucket and walked toward the locker room. My brain couldn't take any more. It wasn't that I just didn't want to be with Chance, I wasn't going to be allowed to be with anyone but Braiden.

****

Following school, I knew I needed to bring my mom up to speed. If I was starting to slip, she would be sure to notice. Dad was still at work, so while my mom was starting dinner, I decided to break the news to her.

"Hey, Mom," I said as I sat down at the dining room table.

"Yes?"

"Can I talk to you for a minute?"

"Sure, sweetie, what's going on?" she asked as she pulled out a chair and took a seat.

"I need to talk to you about something really important," I

told her tracing the wood grain with my fingers and avoiding her concerned eyes.

She looked worried.

"I was supposed to get my period Saturday, but I didn't and I'm not going to."

"You're pregnant?" she finally asked, completely emotionless.

"Yes."

"You're sure?"

"Yes," I said ashamed. "I'm so sorry. I don't know what to do. Please don't tell Dad," I pleaded, still avoiding eye contact.

"Well, I guess that will depend on what you choose to do. "

"I know. Are you mad?"

"No, I'm not mad. Obviously, this isn't what I wanted for you. Children are a blessing, but there's still so much you wanted to do. We can't go back in time and change anything. We need to make the best decision we can now and move forward." I couldn't believe how calm she was.

"What do you think I should do?" I asked, not sure if I wanted to hear her answer.

"It's your decision. Any way you look at it, it changes your life. I just want what's best for you. I love you, but do you really think you're ready for a baby?"

"I don't know. I can't stand the thought of anyone else raising my baby, however I feel like I've run out of options."

"How does Braiden feel about all of this? He knows, doesn't he?"

"Yes. I don't know how to read him. I never know what's going on in his head," I replied, getting up from my chair exasperated. The conversation, the whole situation, had worn me out.

"Krissa, if you abort, you become a Sweeper."

"Yeah, Mom, I know. I can't let that happen."

"Good. I don't want to see you go down that path. I'm sure Headquarters could find the perfect family."

"I'll think about it, okay?"

"I'm sure you'll make the right decision."

I walked to my room agreeing the situation wasn't ideal, but my heart broke to think of the alternatives. I could live with being paired with Braiden, fairly certain we could make it work. I wasn't sure I could live without our baby and was positive I couldn't live as a Sweeper.

****

"What are we going to do?" I asked as Braiden and I sat on his bed watching nothing important on TV after school the next day.

"What do you mean?" He leaned back against the headboard.

"What the hell do you think I'm talking about? We need to talk this out. I know it's uncomfortable, but we put ourselves in this mess."

"I know that, Krissa," he stated agitated.

"Well, where do you stand? What are your feelings about all of this?" I repositioned myself, blocking his view to the screen.

"It's your body, your decision."

"I know you've said in the past, pairing and kids are not what you see in your future, but here we are."

"You're right I didn't want that, but I'm not going to make up your mind for you. What do you want?"

"I don't know. I'm torn up inside. There are pros and cons; my mind tells me one thing while my heart tells another. I'm so confused." Tears rolled down my cheeks. "Becoming a Sweeper is not an option for me."

"Would it really be that bad?"

Stunned by his question, I firmly said, "Yes."

"Why?"

"Because I don't want a Sweepers life! The thought of being paired with you and having our child doesn't scare me. I'd welcome it."

"Krissa, I don't know if I'm ready to be a dad."

"I'm not ready to be a mom. I never wished for this to happen but is forfeiting that right the best choice?" I asked, wiping away my tears.

"This is not our time … but one day it will be." He placed his hand over mine.

"You really want to choose adoption?"

"I think it's best for both of us."

"We'll have to relocate. We can't stay here."

"I don't want to stay here, and neither do you."

"True, but what about the pairing? It's likely they'll pair us."

"We'll cross that bridge when we get to it. It'll all work."

"Promise?"

"Promise."

I couldn't believe what I heard myself agreeing to. I couldn't fathom the fact that I was turning my back on myself, because adoption was never the choice I wanted to make. However, I felt it was the best compromise we'd come to. Not ending up as a Sweeper and being paired with Braiden was good; two out of three wasn't bad.

Ten

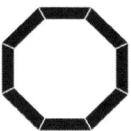

"Hey Mom," I said as I plopped down on her bed.

"Hey honey. How are things going?"

"As good as they can be." I held back my tears. "Braiden and I decided that we aren't going to keep the baby."

"You guys talked it all out, and this is what you really want?" I could tell she didn't believe me, but the expression of relief that washed over her face told me she agreed with our decision.

"It is what it is." I pulled myself off her bed. "I'll contact Headquarters soon," I promised.

Since making our decision, Braiden acted as if everything was fine, more than fine. He acted as if we were no longer in any sort of predicament. I couldn't help but resent him. How was he just okay with everything? He laughed and joked and carried on as if what was to come wasn't bothering him. I felt that to him it was out of sight, out of mind. But it wasn't over for me, not sure it ever would be. He didn't see what he was taking from me. I knew that he was making a compromise too, choosing to become paired, but it still wasn't enough for me. There would always be a missing part of us, and I worried I would forever carry that resentment.

Even though my life felt like it was at a standstill, the world around me kept moving.

"All right girls," I said to the dance team members as we sat in the empty gymnasium hall, "this is our last performance of the year. Thank you all so much for all of your hard work this season and making this such a success. I'm so proud of all we've accomplished. Let's do this last performance right. Have fun out there."

We got up and made our way to the gym. It was the boy's last home basketball game, and the gym was packed. We made our way to the court as the last whistle of the quarter blew.

"Let's do this," Honor said as she and I took our spots in the center of the court. Our last show was a huge hit, and it was a bittersweet end for me. I was on a high from our performance, but in the back of my mind, I knew I was about to hit rock bottom.

"You guys looked great tonight," Braiden said as we made our way to the car.

"Thanks. I can't believe it was our last performance. I'm sad to see it come to an end."

We really didn't have much else to talk about so we got into my car, and I started to drive away. We didn't get very far before I pulled over and placed my head in my hands as I began to sob uncontrollably.

"I can't do it, Braiden. I can't go through with it." Although I knew this would get me nowhere, I couldn't control my emotions. I didn't want to hear all the reasons as to why I was making the right decision, I wanted to hear that he changed his mind. I was hoping by some miracle he realized we were making a mistake.

"You have to, Krissa. We've already made our decision." He was still on board with discarding our child.

"I can't," I managed to say between the tears and hyperventilating. "I can't carry our baby for nine months then give him or her to someone else."

"Calm down. You can do this. You have to do this."

"Please, it doesn't feel right. This is never what I wanted."

"Krissa, you're strong. I know you can do it. There's no other option." I knew there was no turning back and that his decision was final, but I also knew deep down we'd never be the same. How could we be? I'd lost all respect for him. How was I to be paired with someone I hated so much? I felt like he was taking everything from me. This was my first pregnancy, and look at how it was ending. I'd never get another first pregnancy. I was supposed to be excited, yet I was in tears. This wasn't how it was supposed to be.

After an awkward ride, I left Braiden at his house and drove myself home. Crashing in bed, my brain tried to shut off the awful thoughts floating through my it. I drifted off around one in the morning but was suddenly awakened by sharp pains in my abdomen. I tried to force myself back to sleep, but the pain was too intense. I'd never experienced anything quite like it. Quietly I walked into my parent's room and gently tapped my mom on the shoulder.

"Krissa?" She was startled and confused. "What's wrong?" she asked as she got out of the bed.

"My stomach is killing me." I hunched over in excruciating pain.

"What can I do for you?"

"I don't know ... I don't know what's going on. It just really hurts!" I exclaimed.

"Can you make it until the morning to go to Healthcare?"

"No," I said breathing deeply, "I don't think I can."

"Should I take you now?"

"I don't want to go, but what other choice do I have?"

"All right, let's go. I'll leave a note for your father in case he gets home from work and we're not back yet."

I prayed we made it home before he did.

****

The decision was supposed to be mine, but I guess a greater power made the decision for me. I hadn't had the chance to talk to Braiden about the turn of events. We'd left the hospital at 5:30 that morning. I went straight home and crawled into bed. Luckily, we arrived back at the house before my dad made it home from his latest trip. I couldn't face him just yet. I also didn't feel a need to rush to tell Braiden anything either. He'd be relieved. I, on the other hand, was not. I felt as if this was the punishment for the choice I was going to make. I wasn't going to keep the baby, so it made sense to have it taken away. Not getting to meet our child was never the outcome I wanted, but any way you looked at it; the result would've been the same.

I decided to call Braiden at four that afternoon. He'd left messages on my communicator, but I hadn't been ready to re-live what I'd gone through.

"Hello?"

"Hi, Braiden, it's me."

"Where have you been? Why weren't you at school? Is everything all right?" I could tell by the twenty questions he'd been worried, but for the first time, I didn't feel it necessary to put his needs ahead of my own.

I knew this should be a face to face conversation, but I didn't have the emotional strength to confront him. He'd gotten what he wanted, so it was up to me to pick up the mess left behind.

"I don't need to give Headquarters our decision. I miscarried last night. There's no longer a decision to be made."

"What?"

"I spent most of my night at the Healthcare emergency unit."

"What happened?"

I couldn't help but think why he thought it mattered. I was in emotional torment and physical pain. I welcomed the pain because I thought I deserved it and it also distracted me from my thoughts. I answered his questions and did my best to explain everything. "They can't pinpoint why it happened. They told me I didn't do anything wrong and I couldn't have done anything differently to prevent it. These kinds of things just happen."

"So what happens now?"

"What do you mean?" I asked.

"Like, is it all over with? You're no longer pregnant, right? Do you have any restrictions or anything?"

"Yes, it's all over with. I'm fine …. I'll be fine."

"Good. I hate to ask but what happens now with pairing?"

"What do you mean?"

"Well, we don't fall into any category that we talked about with the doctor, so did they tell you what happens after graduation?"

"Wow. That's what you're worried about?"

"Well I feel like I have a right to know what my future looks like."

True. "They're going to pair us. It'd be too difficult to try and explain what happened to a new mate." They acted as if I was damaged goods or something.

"Oh."

"You sound disappointed."

"No, I'm not. I'm just trying to sort it all out."

What was there to sort out? It seemed pretty black and white to me.

"So that's our only option?"

"You can always choose to stay single Braiden. Listen, I'm really tired, can we talk about this later? I'm going to go back to bed."

"Okay. I'm sorry you had to go through all of that, but I'm glad it's all over and you're all right. I'll talk to you later." Braiden hung up the phone. After everything I'd been through, his concerns were still selfish.

The weeks following my miscarriage blurred together and seemed to be insignificant. And while I kept my grades up, I seemed to just exist through school. I slept as much as possible, ate a little as possible and distanced myself from the world, including Braiden. When I tried to talk with him about the miscarriage, he blew it off like it was no big deal. And while I didn't want to go into details of the day, I needed an outlet. I needed to share my feelings with someone. Considering no one knew of our circumstance, I only had his shoulder to cry on, which he didn't offer. I was left to cope on my own.

Lover's Day was upon us, a day adopted by our government from our past that was used to celebrate life and love. It encouraged the pairings, and encouraged individuals to show their love for one another. Braiden and I made plans to celebrate Friday evening. It was the first time we scheduled time together since the mishap. He showed up at my house around seven that evening ready to enjoy a holiday that he saw as a control tactic, government brainwashing at its best. I ignored his negativity.

"Happy Lover's Day," I said as Braiden entered the door.

"Happy Lover's Day to you," he replied as he hugged me. "You know I hate this, right?"

"I know," I murmured, not feeling guilty that I was making

him celebrate. I'd given up too much. And was hoping this holiday would help lift my spirits.

"Come on in. Make yourself comfy."

"Where are your parents tonight?"

"They're out to dinner celebrating this lovely day. Are you hungry? I'm just about finished cooking."

"Yeah, I'm hungry. What did you make?"

"Chicken parmesan."

We sat down at my dining room table to eat the meal I'd prepared, and for the first time in a while, we enjoyed each other's company. Maybe we could be normal again. I mean normal in the sense of high school students' who were just foolishly in love, or like, however you wanted to put it. We looked like normal teenagers who didn't have heavy baggage weighing them down.

"Krissa? You okay?"

"Yeah, fine," I lied. I knew I couldn't talk to him.

"I have something for you." I pushed my chair back away from the table and prompted him to do the same. He followed me to my room where I handed him his gift. He read his card and took the small rectangular box.

"Hurry up, open it," I said excitedly.

"Oh my God! How did you know?"

"You showed it to me once."

"It's awesome. Thank you." He pulled the watch out of the box and placed it around his left wrist.

I wasn't trying to buy his love, but I also knew it couldn't hurt. In the back of my mind I always reassured myself if I did everything right as his girlfriend, he would never consider leaving me.

"I'll be right back. I've got to grab my bag."

I noticed the bag when he first showed up at my house, but I wasn't nosey about it. I'd finally learned to drop my expectations. Love, or at least the word, had come so easily in the past. My first crush told me he loved me soon after dating and Chance told me he loved me from the start. I assumed love would be so easily given this time around, but that was far from true. I wasn't used to chasing after love. I had to re-train my brain to think differently about it. When Braiden re-appeared in my room and pulled out a white stuffed bear that had *I love you* written in red on the bottom of the paws, I overlooked it. I assumed he didn't notice that upon purchasing the bear.

"Thank you. It's adorable." That was the right word for it, adorable, as in, appropriate for a child. I put the bear down careful, not to expose the feet to Braiden. I didn't need him to retract the bear's statement.

"You like it?"

"Yes, I do. Thanks." I knew it sounded selfish, but was that all? It seemed so generic. So … average.

"Did you," he stuttered, "see the feet?"

Startled by the question, I awkwardly replied, "Uh, yeah I did," and avoided his eyes. I didn't want to see the look of embarrassment in them.

"And?"

"And what?" This conversation was getting on my nerves.

"What did they say?"

"I love you," I replied, completely monotone.

"I do."

"Tell me then. I want to hear you say the words."

"I ... I love you."

I pressed my body against his, embracing him. "Thank you for telling me. I love you, too. That was the best present you could've ever given to me. So, how do you feel?" I joked. I felt as if a heavy weight had been lifted.

"Fine. It came out easier than I thought it would," he said confidently.

"It must be the day."

"No, it's not. I love you. I've loved you all along, and I'll continue to love you."

Relief, washed over me. It was crazy how three little words could be so comforting. I knew for certain he'd be in my future. "So you're good with the pairing then?" I knew I was pushing it, but I needed concrete answers.

"I don't want to talk about that tonight."

"Okay. Sometime soon though?"

"Sure." I wasn't sure if he was being serious or sarcastic. He switched the conversation, "That's not all," he reached into his bag for the second time and pulled out a sterling silver bracelet that matched the necklace he'd gotten me for Christmas. It was beautiful, and I loved it—but not nearly as much as I loved hearing him say he loved him. I could see the silver lining; there was finally a light at the end of the dark tunnel I'd been trapped in.

Eleven

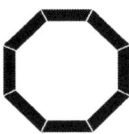

After Lover's Day we finally fell in sync into our relationship. It was where I hoped we'd be all along. I still had my reservations about him since the pregnancy fiasco, but I was trying really hard not to hold a grudge. After all, he did tell me he loved me ... finally. He was going to be my future. I accepted that and was ready to move forward. I thought my heart and mind would finally be at ease. However, it seemed that since he came out with all of his feelings, he felt entitled to treat me even worse than before.

The more candid he was about his feelings, the more degrading he became. I suddenly couldn't do anything right and always felt inferior. The meaner he was, the harder I tried. I wanted to make things better because he was my future. Competing against myself to make him love me more, I felt I needed to give him more to make up for what he wasn't giving me. In retrospect, I was just double dipping out of my own love jar.

While I was happy to move forward with Braiden, my mom well ... wasn't. My mom was more understanding of the whole pregnancy thing than I could have ever hoped for, but over time, her distaste for Braiden evolved. She noticed the changes in me and wasn't fond of the teenager I'd become. She didn't understand my feelings for Braiden and hated even more that I was stuck between a rock and a hard spot when it came to my pairing future.

My dad was on board from the start, but convincing my mom to allow him to accompany us to Headquarters for spring recess was harder than I expected. Hours of begging and pleading were required until she finally caved. We received our consent of travel soon after our request and my excitement heightened immensely as I envisioned my future with Braiden at Headquarters.

We left early Saturday morning to get to the departure tunnel in time. I wasn't a fan of the fast as light shuttle because it made me claustrophobic, but, it was the only way to travel from unit to unit. It was either endure the ride or don't go. Traveling at several hundreds of miles per hour, it took only six hours to travel to Headquarters. It was also easier to make the trip knowing Braiden would be at my side.

The four of us loaded into the four-man compartment and made ourselves comfortable. After putting our bags in the overhead compartment, Braiden and I sat in the two back chairs.

"I'm so excited to go to Headquarters."

"Oh yay, we get to hang out with the controllers. Awesome."

Not amused by Braiden's sarcasm, I wanted to know why he even came if he thought he was going to be miserable, but I wasn't sure I wanted to hear his reasoning, nor did I want to start a fight. "No one forced you to come."

"No, they just put a lot of pressure on me."

"I just thought you'd like to see where I wanted to be, where I'd like us to be. Explore it beyond just the surface information that school provided."

"Whatever," he rolled his eyes. "why do we have to pick one location? Why can't we be free to roam? What's so wrong with being able to go back and forth between units as we see fit? What if we're missing so much? We're so controlled."

"I don't think we're missing anything. We're allowed to visit anywhere we want. As far as the government's control, I think it's for the best. This is the way our country survives and thrives. They keep us safe and provide everything we need. We need to have a government in place, Braiden, that's what makes us successful as a country. We're given the essentials, no one goes without. Yes, we're able to obtain more by working hard, earning money and purchasing more at our own free will, but no one is starving, no one is homeless." Why couldn't he understand that?

"We go when and where they tell us to. It's not fair. Some people are still better off than others. Have you ever seen the Sweeper unit?"

"That unit has acted out against the government. They still have what they need to survive, they just don't get the luxuries. And we have to work hard to get those luxuries too, Braiden; they aren't just handed over. We follow the rules, go to work, we do what's right."

"Exactly. We're only rewarded when we do what the government says we have to do, Krissa. They give us everything they think we need. There's more out there."

"I have everything I need."

"I'm not sure *I* do."

How was I supposed to respond to that? Wasn't I enough? Would I ever be? What if he chose to not be paired? Where would that leave me? I could put Garrett, a family friend that my parents had always rooted for, down on my list, or I could put Chance, but they weren't enough for me.

****

"Wow, this is amazing." He stood next to me on the balcony, twenty-seven stories high at Headquarters.

"Thank you for coming here with me. I'm glad you're here." I leaned my head against his chest.

"You're welcome. You want to go for a walk around the city?" Our hotel was located in the heart of the unit, great for sightseeing.

Given our ride here, I was hesitant. "Sure," I finally answered.

I followed him to the elevator and out onto the street. As I walked beside him, I took note of how amazing he looked in his cargo shorts and V-neck tee, which exposed his perfectly toned body, and glowing skin. He was so hard to resist. It was like my brain was only programmed to remember the good times and automatically filter out all of the bad. A little voice inside my head told me to run as quickly as I could, but I ignored it. And I'd continue to ignore it because I wanted to believe he was good for me and our pairing would fulfill us both.

"What a difference from our unit," he finally said after a long walk in silence.

"Yeah, but I like it," I said as we made our way through the crowded streets.

"It's okay."

"Just okay?"

"It's just crowded," he looked around watching people scurrying into the large, oversized buildings. "And loud. Too hectic for my liking. All I see are tall buildings. There are no trees, no open spaces, it's all concrete and steel. This is really where you want to be?"

It was hard to differentiate if he was curious about it or scolding me. "I think so. There's so much here for me, for us. But I only want to be here if you're here, too."

"I know. We still have a lot of time to decide."

I didn't love his response.

After a few hours of touring, we headed back toward our hotel and the friction that existed between us from earlier faded. I wanted this week to be nothing but positive for Braiden. If that meant not bringing up any tough issues, then I wouldn't. He was right that we still had time before we needed to pick.

"I'm going to take a shower and get ready for tonight," Braiden said as we made our way back to our room.

"I'll get ready when you're done."

I lay on the bed decompressing and decided to check my communicator. I pulled out the small rectangular personal computer and opened up my mail. To my surprise, my inbox had several messages waiting to be opened. Most were spam, but the one that read, *Hope your spring break is going well* in the subject line caught my attention.

My heart stopped for a moment then began to flutter rapidly. I wasn't sure if this was because I was excited Chance had written me or nervous knowing that if Braiden found out, there'd be repercussions. I waited until I heard the shower start before I opened the message. I clicked on the subject line and found a short paragraph from Chance.

To: krissachanning@textileunit.com
From: chancedenton@textileunit.com
Subject: Hope your break is going well.

Kris,

I hope you're enjoying your trip to Headquarters. Everything is the same here, but it's hard for me to think that you're away with him. I know this is inappropriate 1. because you're in a relationship and I really shouldn't be coming in between the two of you and 2. because he's my friend. But I do miss you, and I don't just mean in the sense of distance. He's no good for you. Not that I was great to you either, but I'm going to fight to make it up to you. At least I realize what I've lost, and he doesn't even realize what he has standing right in front of him. Over the past couple of months, I see how he's changed you. I thought I could let you go and move on, but I can't. I've messed up in the past. I won't do that to you in the future, ever. I can make you happy. I can see that you're not happy with him. Let me change that. I've come to realize how important pairing is, and I don't want to remain single. I want a future with you. I'm asking you to pick me. You're going to be my first choice, and I promise we'll be good together. We'll be better than good; we'll be great. We can do whatever, go wherever, I just want to be with you. Please consider what I've said. I love you.

Choose Me.
Chance

I was stunned. I re-read the message two more times to makes sure I comprehended what I was reading. He couldn't be serious! How was I to believe him? He supposedly had a new girlfriend, so he should be considering her as his number one. Not that the word *girlfriend* had any meaning to him. Since I've known Chance, he was never satisfied with the girl he had at the moment, including me. Chance was already given many chances, and I didn't believe he was ready to change.

A part of me was giddy because, well, it was nice to know I

was still wanted. The situation was finally reversed, and now he had a taste of his own medicine. On the other hand, he needed to understand I was over it. He and I would never happen. It wasn't only by my choice but also per the government's rules. I knew my relationship with Braiden wasn't perfect, but I wasn't going anywhere.

"Hey." Braiden startled me as he entered the room unexpectedly. I quickly hit the delete button, and tried to casually put my communicator away. "What are you doing?"

"Just checking my mail. I'm done now," I said, trying to be nonchalant.

"You sure?" he asked suspiciously. "You seemed pretty intrigued with whatever you were doing. I didn't mean to interrupt," he stated defensively.

How long had he been standing there? "No, just deleting my spam messages." I wasn't lying. Chance's email was just that, trash.

"I'm all set to go," he said, sounding slightly irritated.

"I'll go get ready and then we'll head out." I rolled off the bed and made my way to the bathroom, keeping my communicator at my side.

I spent the rest of the night trying to make it up to him although I did nothing wrong, but I still felt ashamed. I wasn't sure if I was guilty because I kept the email from Braiden, or if I secretly liked the fact Chance had written me. I kept telling Braiden how much I loved him and how he meant everything to me, he was my whole life. I wasn't saying anything I didn't mean, but I questioned myself as to who I was reassuring. I knew that I loved Braiden more than anything, but hearing how much I was loved and wanted boosted my confidence. It wasn't often that Braiden told me how much I meant to him; hearing it, even from the wrong person, still felt nice.

****

Our week together passed too quickly. For the most part we got along fine, which meant I only made Braiden angry a few times. I guess it was my fault I let him drink too much which led to him getting sick. I also assumed it was my fault that I didn't steer him away from the piece of glass that cut his foot when he stepped on it. While he kicked me down a few notches, I accepted his words. I would accept the blame as long as it kept him in my life. I was so desperate not to lead a sweeper life that I was willing to give up on myself. Being paired was more important to me than being alone, so I wanted to make him as happy as possible to keep him around. He had the choice to leave, but I'd do everything in my power to get him to stay.

Our final night at Headquarters was upon us. We started off the night by going to dinner accompanied by my parents.

"This is it." My mom looked up at the tall building with a dome-shaped structure on the top.

"Where?" I questioned.

"Up there. Come on." She led us through the building entrance to the glass elevator that quickly climbed to the top.

We stepped off into the most gorgeous restaurant I'd ever been to. The glass dome provided a spectacular view of the city and the twinkling lights below were beautiful.

"Let's sit before I get motion-sick," I urged.

We sat at a square table in the middle of the room under a large blown-glass lighting fixture and nibbled on appetizers as we made small talk about our week.

"Well, Krissa, what are your thoughts about Headquarters," my dad asked as he sipped his beverage.

"It's better than I thought it would be. I really want to be here. I feel like I belong here."

"I think so, too," Mom chimed in. "What about you, Braiden? Do you see yourself here?"

"Mom," I cut in trying to deter her, without success.

"Well?" She turned her attention back to Braiden.

"I'm not sure. I still need to think things over."

"This is what Krissa wants, and her father and I support her decision. If the two of you are paired, you'll have to decide which unit is best."

"I understand, but we do still have some time."

I wished the conversation would just end. I didn't want to discuss this over dinner and quite frankly, I didn't need my mom butting into this matter. This was for Braiden and I to work out. "We'll figure it out, Mom, trust me." I gave her my back off look, and it seemed to work.

We were able to eat and enjoy our dinner without any more

talk about pairing and picking, thank God. It did concern me that even after our visit, Braiden was uncertain. What could I do to make him see this option, with me at Headquarters, was the best one?

"Thank you for dinner. It was great."

"Yes, thank you," Braiden added.

"We're going to take a walk around the city then we'll head back to the hotel, okay?"

"All right," Dad replied. "Don't come back too late. Our shuttle leaves early tomorrow morning."

"No problem." I watched them head off toward the hotel. "Ahh," I let out a big sigh.

"What's wrong?"

"I'm just sad this is our last night here." I grabbed his hand as we made our way down the sidewalk. There were a few people out, but we mostly had the street to ourselves.

"Aren't you kind of glad to get back? You have so much going on."

"I know, I know. I'm excited about all of that," mostly because I got to share all of the upcoming experiences with him, "but being here with you has been such a breath of fresh air." This was exactly how I'd envisioned my future.

Braiden didn't respond to my words, just kept staring off at nothing in particular.

"This trip has been amazing." I broke the silence. "Mostly for the fact you're here to share it with me. I really believe this is the right move for us."

"I know you do."

"I can't wait to get out of our unit. I'll meet new people, see new things and hopefully share it all with you."

"We'll see about that."

"See about what?" I asked anxiously. "Do you not see this for your future?" I was defensive as my heart began to race.

"We have a lot of time to think about things," he said, shifting his attention from me.

"You keep saying that. I don't need any more time to think about anything. Regardless of what my future brings, I know I want you there. Besides," I snapped, laying on the guilt trip, "you promised."

"I know. I'm not saying we won't be together. I'm just saying a lot can happen in the future. What if I don't want to move here? What happens if we can't agree on where to live?"

"Listen," I stated, gazing directly into his eyes, "the most important thing to me is you. If that means I have to give up Headquarters to be with you then I'll do it." I wouldn't be happy about it, yet it seemed like such a small thing to give up in comparison to having him. My parents wouldn't be happy about it either, but it was my life and my decision. "So, where would you want to be?"

"I don't know, Krissa. That's a huge part of my problem. Quite honestly, I don't want to be anywhere the government is."

"Well, I don't think we can avoid that."

"You don't think so?"

"No. I'm not sure if I want to find out if there's a place where they aren't. I'm happy here, Braiden. This makes sense to me."

"How can you be so sure? You don't even know what else is out there?"

"Because I don't think there's anything else out there. I'm happy with the way things are and just wish you were, too. I want this," using my finger to point between us, "to feel right to *you*."

After a moment of silence, he finally returned his attention to me. "We'll figure it out."

"Braiden," I hesitated not sure if I should bring it up, "do you ever think about what would've happened if we didn't lose the baby?"

"That's the past, Krissa. We've moved on."

"I'm trying, but it still haunts me. Not a day goes by that I don't think about the *what if's*."

"You can't think like that. What's done is done. Move forward."

It sounded simple, but was far from easy. "It's easier knowing that you'll be by my side." I tried to sound confident during that statement.

"Come on, let's enjoy our last night here." He swiftly grabbed my arm and pulled me into a barely lit alley way. He pushed me up against the stone wall, kissing me passionately while his hands moved across my body.

"What are you doing? We're going to get caught. I don't think this is a good idea." My brain was using logic, but my body kept asking for more.

"It's fine, there's no one around."

I remembered the last time he told me we weren't going to get caught, and while he didn't, I did. I still hadn't told him about my encounter with the Enforcer at the dance. I didn't want to add anything else to his plate, but I didn't need them watching this act either. "Braiden, stop. I don't want to get into trouble."

"You won't."

Before I could argue anymore, he already had my dress up. Our session was short lived, thankfully, and we didn't manage to attract any attention.

"See, I told you," he snickered. He grabbed my hand and led me back toward the hotel.

I glanced over my shoulder making sure no one had seen us in the act and was relieved to find the street empty. However, right before I turned my head back, a shiny silver speck caught my eye. A street camera was placed right above where we'd just been. My heartbeat picked up as anxiety crept in. I didn't need another ding against me. I wanted a clean record to keep my chances of getting to Headquarters the best it could be. I kept my fingers crossed that Headquarters missed our rendezvous, but I was warned they were watching.

Twelve

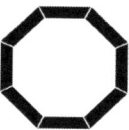

Our break was short lived, but amazing. It was time to face reality and go back to our everyday high school lives. By the time I reached fitness class, I'd heard all about my friends' week and it was time to face the one situation I'd been trying so hard to avoid.

"All right everyone, you know the drill. After you run or walk a mile, you're free to do as you please out here. I'll be watching," Mrs. Staunton said as the class gathered outside on the rubber track. Suddenly, I felt a hand on my shoulder tugging me to turn around. I did a one-eighty and came face to face with Chance.

"Welcome back," he said enthusiastically.

"How are you?" I was trying to be nice.

"I'm good. How was your time in Headquarters?"

"Great, I'm pretty sure that'll be my first pick."

"I like it there, too, and I would go there especially if you were there." He had to throw that in, but I ignored his comment. He hesitated. "I wrote you an e-mail last week." The whistle blew, indicating our mile had to begin. I hoped running would distract him enough he wouldn't wait for me to respond.

No such luck. "Kris?"

"What?" Our feet thudded against the track in rhythm.

"Did you get my message?"

"You know what? I didn't have a chance to check my mail while we were away. Braiden and I were out and about the whole time." He swiftly grabbed my hand and pulled me off the track.

"Chance! What are you doing?" I exclaimed, trying to resist his tugging.

"Just come with me, please." He continued to drag me along.

"No! We're going to get in trouble. Let go," I said, trying to release my wrist from his grip.

He stopped once we were hidden behind the bleachers. "Look, I love you, Kris. I hate seeing you with him. He doesn't treat you well."

"Neither did you," I blurted out. Why did I care? He didn't even deserve a response. "Braiden's your friend. You can't be saying these things."

"You're right. But you were mine first, and I'm sorry I ever let you go."

"I'm not sorry."

"I messed up. I know!" he said desperately while grabbing my shoulders, holding me in place.

"Let go, Chance."

"No. I'm not letting go of you." I knew he meant more than his grip.

"Chance—" I was cut off when he pressed his lips against

mine. I tried to pull away, but his grip around my arms only tightened. Yes, my lips were against his, but I wasn't kissing back. Eventually, he pulled away and I stared at him in disbelief.

"No, Chance!" I ripped my arms away and folded them across my chest as if protecting myself against another one of his attacks. "Never. We will never happen! Why don't you understand that? We are over. We've been over. I love Braiden. Braiden is my first pick, he is my only option." I was direct and harsh, but after his daring move, he needed to hear it, loud and clear.

"I'm not giving up." He headed back to the track.

"Eventually you will. You can't wait around forever."

He looked back over his shoulder grinning. "You guys won't last forever." And then he was gone.

He knew his words would hurt me. Why was he doing this? He didn't want Braiden hurting me, yet here he was trying to destroy the only thing I wanted.

I wasn't returning to gym class, so I walked back to the locker room and changed. I didn't want to see Chance again, and I was so angry. The more I thought about it, I wasn't sure if I was more angry because he kissed me or if it was because he was so sure that Braiden and I wouldn't last. What if he was right? He planted a seed in my head that I never wanted to see grow.

Luckily, I was able to avoid the next two fitness classes. We had our senior meeting one day and the next we went to a unit conference where leaders from around the country set up booths to promote their units.

We were sectioned off when we entered the gym, leaving me without Chance or Braiden. I didn't mind though, Honor and Hope were with me as we walked around the path. We stopped at each booth as we were told, reviewed each unit's information and heard their pitch, but the three of us were already set on where we wanted to be placed.

The Finance district was too stuffy, the Cares endured too much schooling and the Engineers didn't seem to have too much fun. The Agriculture and Builders units were never an option. They were both labor intensive, and I was not up for that challenge.

"That was fun," Honor said.

"I'm exhausted. That was a lot to take in," Hope stated. "Some of the other units looked promising, but I just can't see myself away from here."

"Me either," Honor said.

I looked at both of them in shock. I didn't understand how they didn't want to venture out. I loved our unit, but needed something more.

"Did you guys notice the Sweeper unit wasn't represented?" I asked my friends.

"Why would it be?" Hope responded.

"It's an option," I countered.

"Not a good one."

"True." How could Braiden think there was quality life in that unit? "What are you plans for the weekend? Anything special?"

"I'm going to Emery's game, he's pitching," Honor said as she chewed on candy she pulled out of her bag.

"That will be fun," I joined in. "What about you, Hope?" I grabbed a piece of chocolate.

"Noble's family is coming from the finance unit; his dad is hosting a dinner party."

"Is this the first time you're meeting them?" Honor asked curiously.

"I've talked with them on the communicator before, but I've never met them."

"Are you nervous?" Honor continued with her questions.

"Not really. Noble says they'll love me, so I'm taking his word for it."

"I'm sure they will," I reassured her.

"So, Kris," Honor began, popping another piece of chocolate into her mouth, "how are things with you and Braiden? You seem to be getting along better."

"Yeah," I answered really uncomfortably. These girls were my best friends and it'd been hell trying to keep things from them, lie to them. "We had a rough patch, but everything worked itself out." I guess that was the best explanation. "Everything is great now. We had a good time at Headquarters."

"Will that be his pick?" Honor continued on.

"I hope so. We haven't talked about it much."

"Why not?"

"It's Braiden. He doesn't like the whole concept of pairing and picking, but he'll have to do it eventually, right?"

"I guess. I mean he could always choose to remain a Single." The thought tore at my heart. "Is he really the best pairing for you?"

I didn't have an option, but I was fine with that. The only way I would have a choice would be if he chose the Single's unit. Suddenly, I couldn't bear the thought. "Yes. I love him and want to spend my life with him."

"Do you have other choices?"

"I'm going to put down two other options," not like it mattered, "but I'm banking on being paired with him."

With nothing else to say on that matter, Hope changed the subject. I was in on the conversation but only picked up bits and pieces. Joy and Gabriel were hoping to be placed in the Educator unit while Charity and Victor were arguing about which unit was best. I vaguely heard what was being said as I was in my own head, worrying what my future might look like.

I headed home that night realizing it wouldn't be long until my senior year would come to an end. The senior convention had kicked off all of the senior moments that I'd been waiting for, and now I felt as if I'd wished my whole senior year away. Everything was coming to an end. I wanted everything to fall into place and work out so badly, but a small part of my brain couldn't let go of the fact that my future lay in the hands of another.

Four more weeks until my graduation and every weekend was packed with events. Tonight was our end of the year dance, which allowed all grades to attend. Considering I made the majority of the plans for the senior exit dance, I wanted to do what Braiden wanted, even if that meant hanging out with his friends. On the brighter side, at least Chance wasn't going to be with us. I'd been trying my best to keep my distance since the kissing incident, and I'd been doing a pretty good job.

During fitness class, I made myself unavailable at all times, keeping myself surrounded by friends and avoided all eye contact with Chance. All of the required subjects had been covered so we were able to pick what we wanted to do. I chose to play football a couple of times when Chance had opted out of the game, but I was frustrated when only one younger kid, Duke, would include me. Discouraged, I settled for tennis with the girls keeping the distance between Chance and me. My biggest hope was that I'd be as successful avoiding him at the dance.

Thirteen

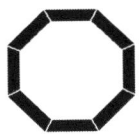

The evening started out at my house with picture taking.

I walked out of my room to find my mom standing in the hallway. "Oh, Krissa, you look amazing."

"Thank you." I kissed her cheek and proceeded outside where Braiden and my dad waited patiently. Walking steadily in my strappy stilettos, my body hugging dress, which was short in the front and long in the back, swooshed behind me. I caught Braiden's eye and couldn't help but smile. He looked divine.

"You look amazing," Braiden stated as I stepped outside.

"Come on over here guys," my dad said, suggesting pictures under the willow tree.

After a sufficient amount of shots were taken, we were ready to head out.

"Thanks for taking all of the pictures Dad, but we need to head over to Braiden's now." I grabbed my overnight bag.

"See you tomorrow. Love you!"

"Love you, too," Mom said.

"Have a great time," my dad called out as I drove away.

"Your grandparents are at your house, right?" I asked Braiden, pulling out of my driveway.

"Yep. They're very excited to meet you. My mom's been telling them all about you."

"I hope only good things."

"I'm sure. She's so excited that I have a girlfriend, she tells everyone about our business."

"Well I'm excited to meet them too." Another monumental moment in our relationship.

We pulled up to his house around 6:30 and his mom was waiting for us in the driveway. Grace greeted us and led us to the backyard.

"You must be Krissa," an older woman said as I approached. "Grace has told me a lot about you. She didn't do you justice in her description though. My goodness, you're beautiful."

"Thank you." I was embarrassed. "It must be the dress," I told her as I swayed back and forth letting the sun radiate off the iridescent beads.

"No," Braiden interjected, "you look this beautiful every day." Sometimes I believed I dated two Braidens. The first Braiden didn't appreciate me while the second Braiden said such amazing, loving words. He seemed to cast me off when he didn't want me, but reel me in at his convenience.

"Krissa, you look gorgeous." Grace stood by my side. "As you probably figured, this is my mother, Ada."

"It's very nice to meet you," I said as I extended my hand.

"It's nice to be able to put a face to a name," Ada said as she took my hand. She was older than I expected. She looked tiny and frail, but her energy was high. Many delicate lines covered a face I could tell was once flawlessly beautiful. Behind the lines was light, creamy, delicate skin. Her now silver hair was pulled into a bun pinned at the top of her head, and her piercing green eyes were the most prominent feature on her face. It was clear to me, many of Braiden's features came from his mother's side. I supposed, to him, that was a good thing. I imagined it'd be hard to wake up every day and be reminded of someone that walked out on you every time you looked into the mirror.

"And this is my father, Alexander."

"Well it's about time I got to meet the girl who's tamed that grandson of mine." I couldn't help but smile at the thought.

"It's nice to meet you as well." I extended my hand out for the second time. Instead of a handshake, I was pulled for a bear hug.

"Gramps, let her go," Braiden grumbled behind me. He gave me another tight squeeze and then released his grip. I took a step back, looked up at Alexander and smiled. It was a wonderful feeling to be accepted by his family.

"What a welcome," I said. One thing I was sure of was while Braiden got his looks from his mom's family, he definitely didn't get his emotional essence from that side.

"How about some pictures?" Grace asked after introductions.

"Really, Mom? We just took a ton at Krissa's."

"Well, I want some, too. Why do her parents get to have all the fun?"

"She's right," I said as I turned to Braiden.

"Just amuse me, Braiden." His mom pulled out her camera.

"Fine," Braiden huffed. "Where do you want us to stand?" he asked, sounding unamused.

"Over there." She pointed.

I took Braiden's hand and led him across their yard to stand in front of their aesthetically pleasing water well.

"Say cheese," Grace called as she snapped several pictures.

"That's enough, Mom," Braiden complained dramatically.

A few more rounds of picture taking and Braiden called it quits.

"You kids have a good time," Leon said as Braiden and I made our way back to the car.

"Call me tomorrow and let me know what your plans are. Have fun, thanks for coming over," Grace said, waving.

"It was nice to meet you." I directed my look toward Ada and Alexander.

"It was our pleasure. See you again soon," they said, smiling.

"Hopefully," I replied then shot Braiden a glance.

"Sorry about my gramps," Braiden said once we were alone.

"I didn't mind. He was cute. At least they liked me," I replied, grinning.

"Almost too much."

"What do you mean?"

"Now, they're going to drill me like crazy about pairing."

"And that's a bad thing? Us pairing?"

"Just a lot of pressure."

"Everyone is under the same pressure and quite honestly, it doesn't seem we have a choice when it comes to the pairing. It's been made easier for us. "

"It's just all coming so fast. I hope I'm ready." For my sake, I hoped so, too.

We made our way to meet everyone at Fresca's for dinner. We were the last to arrive. The hostess guided us through double glass doors to a long table where the rest of our party sat.

"What's going on?" Braiden asked all of his friends as we approached. The last two chairs still unclaimed sat beside Hope and Noble. Although Braiden made the majority of the plans, I insisted on inviting them. I considered them my saving grace.

"Hey, Krissa, I saved these seats for you guys."

Thanks for saving me, I thought. It's not that I didn't like Braiden's friends, because I really didn't know them that well, I was just more comfortable with my own friends. "You look amazing," I told her as I claimed the seat closest to her. Her knee-length pink dress accentuated her slender figure.

"Thanks. You look great, too."

I caught Noble's attention and understood the look he was giving me. "You look handsome, too," I stated, soothing his ego.

The other girls looked stellar, but my attention was on Braiden. He was so attractive. I still didn't understand how people saw us differently, as if we still didn't fit together. It's true, he was far from my type and we didn't' run in the same social circles, but he fascinated me. He was my Rubik's cube. There were so many pieces to him that I was still trying to match up. I hoped that I was the one who got to figure him out, to solve his puzzle.

"So," Hope interrupted, "are you guys going to Pax's house afterwards?"

"Yeah, that's the plan." I rolled my eyes.

"You apparently aren't in favor?" Hope asked me when the table's attention was elsewhere.

"It's all of his friends, which is fine, but I don't really fit in with them."

"You mean they don't fit in with you."

I giggled. "I guess. What are you doing after the dance?"

"Going to Noble's house. His dad is gone for the weekend."

"Lucky."

"You rented a room for tonight, right? What did you tell your mom?"

"I told her you and I were getting a hotel room after the dance."

"All right, well, I'll remember that if I'm asked," she said, agreeing to stick to my storyline. "What our parents don't know won't kill them."

"How's your dinner?" Braiden asked interrupting. I didn't mind, Hope had been monopolizing most of my time since we sat down.

"It's good. What about yours?"

"Good. Are you almost ready to head to Pax's?"

"Sure." I was glad dinner was coming to an end. Hope and Noble were ready to head out, and I was ready to get to Pax's. I wanted to get to the dance as quick as possible, cutting the time with his friends as much as I could. The boys were immature and the girls were very different from my friends. Conversations didn't run smoothly with them. I felt like I was being watched more than I was being conversed with. It was awkward.

After dinner six of us headed over to Pax's house. There was going to be drinking involved; therefore, Noble took the responsible route and removed himself and Hope from the situation. We pulled up to a two-story, white vinyl house with a brick arched doorway. "All right, everyone," Pax said, making his way to the bright open kitchen, "what would you all like to drink?"

Braiden, Pax, and Tobin started off the night with shots of Jameson, while Pax and Tobin's dates sipped on fruity mixed drinks.

"You're not drinking?" Tobin asked, shocked.

"I'm good right now. Thanks."

"Suit yourself. You guys want another?" He turned to his friends and grabbed the whisky bottle off of the counter. They took another shot, then a third, sucking in air after downing the liquid that was sure to burn on its way down.

I walked over to Braiden and whispered in his ear, "Don't get too drunk. I'd like you to actually remember tonight."

"No worries," he reassured me. He pulled off his blazer and headed toward the bottle, shot glass in tow. After the fourth round of shots, the boys switched to a game of beer pong while the girls topped off their cups.

"You're not drinking?" Pax's date, Mercy, asked as she approached the bar area where I was sitting.

"No, I'm the designated driver tonight, thank God," I said as I rolled my eyes toward the exciting match of beer pong.

"Boys can be so dumb."

"Tell me about it."

"I really like your dress." She took a seat on the barstool next to me.

"Thank you," I said awkwardly, readjusting my skirt.

"I wish a dress would fit me like that." A dress like mine wouldn't work on her. She was too short and not well endowed in the chest area like I was. "Braiden's lucky to have you."

I smiled at her uncomfortably. "Um, thanks." I hadn't talked with Mercy much, so for her to be dishing out compliments was odd to me.

"I mean it. You're in the most popular group at school, plus you could have just about any guy, yet he got the chance to be with you."

"I guess so." I was fidgeting in my chair trying to get comfortable, but the conversation taking place was really uncomfortable.

"Seriously," she continued, "all of my friends talk about how unlikely your relationship is."

"Wait," I said, stopping her, "why do you talk about us? I've dated someone else in your circle of friends, why is Braiden any different?"

"You and Chance meshed well. He's a player, outspoken, thinks highly of himself and he's hot. All of the girls want him. We weren't surprised that he landed you."

"And Braiden is different how?" I asked, becoming a little annoyed at where this conversation was going. I wasn't sure if I was getting angry because they were dissing Braiden, or if they were making fun of me for choosing someone *below my standards*.

"Well," she started, and then stopped, realizing she might be beginning to offend me.

"Well, what?"

She started apprehensively, "Braiden's never put himself out there, never had a girlfriend. We actually thought he'd never be paired." Little did she know, that was still a possibility. "Then he snagged you. We were all surprised, but honestly, no one really noticed him until you guys started dating. Now, he's noticed."

"He may get more attention, but he's not available." I sounded confident, but certainly didn't feel it.

"Doesn't mean they won't try."

"What do you mean by that?" I tried to sound curious instead of jealous.

"I've just heard some girls saying inappropriate things about him."

"Classy." I tried to keep my voice even.

"Harmony is the worst, though." Her name wasn't fitting.

"Isn't she a year younger? She's still a year off from pairing."

"I know. You have nothing to worry about. Braiden would be a fool to choose her over you."

"I hope you're right." I looked over at Braiden as he flashed me that devilish grin that rattled every bone in my body. Another year out from pairing wasn't seen as a positive, but given Braiden's aversion to pairing, he might view that as a good thing.

"Well, I think we should get to the dance before it ends," I said, standing up from the barstool. "It was really nice talking with you." She gave me much more than I expected and I appreciated her insight on things, even if I suddenly felt a little threatened.

"I'm ready," Braiden said sloppily as he walked slightly off balanced toward me.

"Let's go." We got into my car and made our way to the banquet hall where the dance awaited us.

"What were you and Mercy talking about?" I didn't want to have him even entertain the idea of another girl courting him.

"She complimented my dress then asked me some questions about us." I didn't lie, I just didn't tell the whole truth.

"What kind of questions."

"Nothing major. Girl talk." I changed the subject as quickly as possible. "So ... did you have fun?" I asked, trying to be inconspicuous about the change in conversation.

"You're looking at the beer pong champ."

"I'm so proud," I said sarcastically as I gave him a few slaps on the knee.

We pulled up to the farm-like establishment that doubled as a restaurant on one end and a banquet room at the other. It was a large, white stone structure trimmed in brown with an angled roof. We walked up the cement steps, went through the large wooden door, and made our way to the room that held the majority of the student body. We were stopped right after entering the door for a picture.

"A little closer. Perfect. Smile." The camera flashed. "Fill out the sheet please so you can review and order pictures on your communicator," said the older photographer. "Next!"

"Thank you," I said as Braiden pulled me through the sea of students. Considering it was a dance for all grades, the facility was packed. Braiden wasn't usually one to encourage our way on the dance floor, but tonight he wasn't thinking clearly. With a little liquid courage, he was washed over with dance fever.

After playing several upbeat pop songs, they finally slowed it down. "I'm dying of thirst," Braiden said during the second slow song.

"Go grab us something to drink. I need to go to the bathroom anyway. I'll find you."

"Okay. I'll be over there," he pointed to the tables nearest the refreshments. I made my way around the corner and down the hall toward the restroom when I felt a tug on my wrist. I turned, thinking Braiden had followed me, but was taken by surprise when Chance stood before me.

"Oh, hey Chance," I said surprised.

"Hey Kris. I saw you walking this way and thought I'd meet up with you to tell you that you look really great." His eyes scanned my body.

"Err, thanks." I wrapped my arms around my mid-section, trying to hide myself from his stares. "You look nice, too. Have you had a good time tonight?" I asked, trying to keep it casual.

"Yeah."

"That's good. I've got to get going. Braiden's waiting for me."

I turned to walk the couple of remaining feet to the bathroom when Chance grabbed my shoulder, turning me around and pulling me into him. "I'm not giving up," he whispered in my ear before he kissed my cheek. I watched him walk away while I still felt the warmth of his lips against my cheek. I quickly looked around, hoping no one noticed our encounter then ducked into the bathroom to regain my composure. He still thought he owned me and could do as he pleased. It was not okay for him to talk to me like that, let alone kiss me whenever he wanted.

After getting myself together, I made my way back past the dance floor to the beautiful tables covered in baby blue tablecloths with silver candles grouped in the center. I found Braiden easily through the crowd; he was facing me talking with someone as I approached the table. As I got closer, I realized it wasn't just anyone talking with him, it was Chance. What was he doing there? Couldn't he just let us be?

"Hey Kris. You look nice tonight." He was actually pretending what took place down the hall a few moments ago never happened. How could he hold up this boldface lie right in front of his so called best friend? "So what do you think?" he asked, showing himself off.

"Nice outfit." I was irritated.

"Thanks." He seemed disappointed with my response.

"Not nearly as nice as mine," Braiden interjected. I turned to Braiden and winked, agreeing with his statement.

"Time to dance?" I asked, reaching for Braiden's hand, trying to break up the love triangle I hated to be in the middle of. Unfortunately, before Braiden had the chance to lock hands with mine, Chance felt the need to intercept.

"Sure, I'd love to."

He was annoyingly persistent. I retracted my arm. "Braiden and I arrived not long ago, I'd like the chance to dance with him some more."

"That's cool," he said, trying to disguise his disappointment. "Save one for me later?"

I felt a hint of jealously radiating off of Braiden, but he kept his mouth shut.

"Maybe." There was no way. The night belonged to Braiden; I belonged only to him.

****

We took in the beautiful night as we walked to my car. The air was refreshing, fresh air that was coming in for the summer. Everything was in bloom: full trees, colorful flowers, our relationship.

"Ugh. I'm sweating," Braiden proclaimed as he took off his jacket and slung it over his shoulder.

"And your sweat smells like alcohol," I said using my thumb and pointer finger to pinch the end of my nose.

"I'm not that bad," he stated while using both hands to waft his scent toward me. "You love it."

I shot him a look, and he knew I couldn't argue with that. I loved everything about him, even if he did reek like the bottom of an aged whiskey bottle.

"Think you'll be able to compose yourself so we can have some more fun?" I asked him while trying to keep a straight face.

"Hell yes."

We couldn't get to the hotel quickly enough. I waved the motel key in front of the small automatic lock and waited for the click. I pulled down on the door lever a moment later and opened the door to our love chateau.

"Where'd you put the cooler we brought earlier?" I asked.

"Next to the dresser." He pointed to the only dresser in the room.

I walked through the small motel room, unimpressed by the light cream and pink wallpaper, multicolored floral bedspread and outdated furniture. I didn't pay for high quality; it wasn't like we were here for the service, so I didn't pay much mind to the condition of the cheap room. I grabbed the liquor bottle out of the cooler in attempt to catch up to Braiden's state of mind. As he reached for a shot glass to go round for round with me, I realized that wasn't going to happen. After several shots, I figured it was time to slip out of my dress and into something more comfortable.

"Can you unzip my dress please?" I walked over and turned my back to him. He did as I asked and led the zipper down my lower back. Air tickled my bare skin. "Thank you," I said as I held my straps in place, not allowing my dress to fall to the floor.

I began to walk past him toward the bathroom to change, but he blocked me. He stood in front of me wearing the diabolic grin I knew all too well. He placed his hands over mine and removed them from the delicate straps. My dress slipped off of my body, beads rattling as my dress hit the floor. He placed his hands in the nooks of my collarbone and drew me closer to him. His lips met mine with enthusiasm, and I was just as eager. I quickly unbuttoned his shirt and tore it off. We shuffled toward the bed as one and as the back of my legs found the edge of the bed, I hurled our bodies onto the king sized mattress.

My head was swirling slightly, and I wasn't sure if it was from the alcohol or my raging hormones. As Braiden lay on top of me, his motions began to slow, teasing me for more.

He suddenly paused. "What's wrong?" I asked, surprised and confused.

He stared me dead in the eyes, as if trying to see through me. "I love you so much."

"I know you do." I was fairly certain he did, he just wasn't the best at showing it.

"You're my life."

Braiden never spoke like this. He never fully expressed himself, never let himself be this unguarded. He told me he loved me months back, but I never knew if there were any feelings to support the words. Most of the time, they felt empty and were uttered only in response to when I told him I loved him first. These words had depth. They had meaning.

"I love you so much, and I plan on doing that forever."

"I can let you do that." He suffocated my mouth with his.

That was unexpected. Finally, he saw himself with only me, forever. A wave of relief washed over me knowing what my future looked like.

We woke up in the late morning, feeling the repercussions of our binge drinking. "Good morning." I covered my mouth to keep my stale breath from reaching him.

"Good morning," he replied back, stretching out his perfect body.

"Did you sleep well?" I asked, trying to stop the swirling in my head.

"I passed out well," he chuckled.

"We need to pack up. Check out is in a half hour."

We packed our belongings picked up the room that looked as

if a small tornado had touched down in the middle of the night, and checked out with two minutes to spare.

"All right, we're all set." I climbed into the driver's seat. "You ready?"

"Yup."

As I drove to Braiden's house, I contemplated bringing up the drunken conversation we had for sober confirmation, but I hesitated. It's not that I didn't want to trust him, but our whole relationship he opposed the pairing, what changed? Did I really want to know if he meant what he said? I pulled up to the front of his house and decided to let him be the first to bring it up.

"Thanks for a great night."

"You're welcome, and thank you," he said with a wink. "I'll see you tomorrow." He exited the car.

I rolled down the window. "Sounds good." He began to walk towards his house. "I love you," I called out to him.

He turned around flashed me his perfect smile. "I know you do," he said confidently then disappeared through his front door.

Fourteen

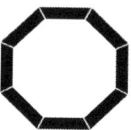

With only ten days left, school was breezing by and my classes no longer required work. I was far more concerned about my weekend events than what was going on throughout the week. Most recently, I'd been focused on the eleven dance numbers for my recitals. I had a large audience to impress. Not only were Braiden and his parents coming Saturday, but my grandparents were granted permission to travel from the Educator unit to come.

Friday night's show was amazing, but I was most nervous for Saturday's performance. Aside from Braiden's family and mine, Honor, Emery, Hope, Noble, and Joy were all there to support me.

"Go Krissa! Wooooooooooo!" I heard Joy scream from the audience. I cracked a smile and giggled.

"Go Kris!" I heard Chance yell over the silence from the front right corner of the audience. I'm sure that will go over real well with Braiden sitting out there in the sea of people. Just then the music started and my brain switched to thoughts of the dance steps rather than the screaming that just rang through me.

All of my hard work paid off and the endless hours of perfecting practice were worth the flawless recital I performed.

"You were fabulous dear," my grandmother, Irene, told me as she handed me a large bouquet of flowers. I idolized my grandmother. She was such an amazing woman and always carried herself with such class. Her impeccable style combined with her poise gave me something to work toward. Her clothes were sensational and her dark grey hair was always set in perfect curls. She took pride in her appearance, but never criticized anyone else's. I hoped one day I could be an amazing woman like her.

"I don't know how you remembered all of the moves," my grandfather, Earnest, said. My grandfather was still handsome. His full head of snow white hair gave the appearance of a darker complexion than what he really had. He had a joy and passion for life and showed it by wearing a large, everlasting smile.

"I'm not sure either! I'm just glad I didn't mess up," I told them, pleased with my performances. As I continued to gloat, Chance somehow managed to push his way through everyone to meet me.

"Hey Kris." Chance stopped in front of me. I looked around, hoping Braiden wasn't near. "You looked great out there," he said as he placed his arm around my waist and leaned in to kiss me on my cheek.

"Thanks." I quickly backed away, releasing his hand from my side. Just as I did, I noticed Braiden out of the corner of my eye looking around the crowd trying to locate me.

"Braiden!" I called loudly as I threw my arm up in the air making my presence known.

"You were great!" Braiden stated as he approached me, pink roses in his hand.

"She was, wasn't she?" Chance interjected.

"Way to support my girl out there," Braiden said territorially as he handed over the flowers and gave me a gentle kiss on the cheek. I saw the look of defeat on Chance's face when Braiden kissed me.

"You heard that?" Chance asked, knowing damn well everyone heard it.

"You're a dumbass," Braiden joked with him. And while he kept his cool on the outside, I knew him better than that. The way he locked his jaw and closed his eyes a little tighter when he spoke, led me to believe he wasn't as enthusiastic about Chance's remarks as he claimed to be.

"Just pumping her up for the big show," Chance said, followed by obnoxious laughter.

"I think she would have done fine regardless." Finally! Braiden was calling Chance out on his bullshit. I was tired of being the one taking the heat.

"Hey Braiden," I pulled him around towards my family. "I want to introduce you to my grandparents. This is my grandmother Irene and my grandfather Earnest."

My grandmother spoke first. "It's nice to meet you Braiden.

Krissa has told us so much about you."

"All good things, I hope."

"Of course," my grandmother answered with a warm smile.

"It's nice to meet all of you, but I've got to run. My parents are waiting for me."

"Thank them for coming, especially Leon for enduring two hours of dance." I kissed his cheek and sent him off. "See you tomorrow."

****

"Hey!" I was excited about Braiden's arrival the next day. He made his way on to the deck where we sat around the glass patio table. "We were just about to start grilling, what would you like?"

"A burger is fine," he said glancing over at my dad who was standing in front of his beloved, top of the line grill that he'd worked so hard for.

"So, Braiden," Dad began, "What did you think of the show last night?"

"It wasn't my sort of thing, but Krissa did great."

"Aww thanks," I said nudging him. I felt so at ease. The past year had its challenges and I still mourned our baby, but I was moving forward. I accepted the loss and tried to see the positives it had brought. I had everything I wanted. I had a wonderful family and the boy who completed me. My grandparents just celebrated their fiftieth year paired, and I envied what they had. They were proof pairing worked and worked well. I always wished to find my perfect half, like my grandparents had found, and sitting around the table looking at how wonderful everything around me was, I realized I might have found just that. I imagined Braiden and I in our seventies with gray hair and wrinkled skin, with eyes that still burned with passion for one another. I seemed to let go of my fear of the future and accept it with open arms, anticipating that many years from now, the possibility of Braiden and I sharing our fiftieth year paired was very real.

The rest of the day flew by with more questions, laughs and storytelling. Before long, my family needed to get back to their unit before curfew.

"Thank you guys so much for coming. It was so great to have your support. I love you."

"We wouldn't have missed it. Love you too, sweetie," my grandma said.

"Love you. Good luck with the rest of school. See you in a few weeks," my grandpa said as my mom pulled away with them in tow.

"Bye!" I watched the car drive away feeling so grateful for all the love that was in my life. Everything was perfect.

Fifteen

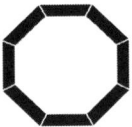

Our last full week of school was upon us; it was bittersweet. The students spent much of their time trading class books and writing wishes to friends as they ventured into the next phase of their lives while the teachers tried hard to get the last preparations in for final exams.

While it was good to see the finish line, I was apprehensive about leaving the unit. What would become of my high school friends? Would we remain close? I was never a fan of high school per se, but I enjoyed the relationships that were built in the establishment. Would I create the same bonds in my new unit? Or was this a one-time deal? My biggest worry was what would come of my uncommon relationship. I knew there was nothing out there that could live up to what Braiden and I shared, but I had to face the future head on.

On Friday the last bell rang, and aside from one last test, freedom was upon us. The last bell solidified the end for us seniors. It was time to party. Our much-anticipated exit dance was the following night in the banquet hall of our City Center. I was looking forward to the dance and had the perfect dress, the perfect date, and the company of my best friends.

Dance had ended, so I had plenty of time to get ready. Honor, Hope and I met at the salon for one more bronzing session before getting perfect manicures and beautiful up-do's. We agreed to meet back at my house to get ready and have pictures taken. Our black stretch automobile—provided by the government for special occasions—would be picking us up at eight o'clock that night.

"Krissa," my mom yelled from the living room, "the girls are here."

I finished picking up my room and made my way to greet my guests. "Hey girls," I said excitedly as I reached them. "Ready to get started?"

"Yeah," Hope said as she carried her dress in a white garment bag toward my room.

"I'm ready," Honor replied as she carried her dress in one arm and a large tote filled with makeup in the other. Even though Honor was low maintenance, she had a gift for doing makeup. Hope and I both jumped at the chance when she offered to do our makeup for the evening.

"Well," my mom began, "we'll be on the deck while you girls get ready," meaning my parents, accompanied by Hope's and Honor's parents, were going outside to indulge in alcoholic beverages.

"Enjoy," I said enthusiastically before darting off to my room.

"Okay, who's first?" Honor asked.

"Hope, you can go first," I said while I pulled out my dress from my closet. "I'm going to get dressed."

"All right."

"That dress looks amazing!" Honor said as she finished Hope's makeup.

"Yeah Krissa, it's gorgeous."

"Thanks, guys." I gave myself a glance in the mirror as I twirled around in the dress my dad had to work extra hours for. The form-fitting bodice accentuated my hourglass figure. I finished off my look with several thin, gold bangles on my right arm, a jeweled gold necklace and strappy gold stilettos.

"Okay, Kris, your turn," Honor said.

"I'm ready."

Honor worked quickly and diligently, and the outcome was fantastic. Hope finished getting ready, putting together a knockout look.

"You look gorgeous, Hope," I said, checking out her ensemble.

"Thanks. I think so." She flashed us a smile.

"Give me a few minutes, and I'll be ready for pictures," Honor told us.

"We can get a few in before the guys show up," I told them.

Ten minutes later Honor was finished, looking breathtaking in her royal blue dress. We headed out the back sliding glass doors to our parents, who patiently waited with cameras glued to their palms.

"Over here, girls," my dad said as we smiled for another round. "That should do. Just a few more when your dates get here and we'll be set."

"Thanks, Dad."

We waited a few more moments for our dates while our sappy parents gushed over how grown up we were. Emotions were running high when our dates arrived, especially mine considering I was the only one in that group who planned on relocating.

Emery was the first to get dropped off by his older sister, Noble showed up next, and Braiden showed up last with his mom.

"You look very handsome," I told him, checking him out in his black tuxedo. He could wear a paper bag and he'd look fabulous.

"Yippee," he responded sarcastically. I knew dressing up and dances were not his thing so I accepted the sarcasm in stride.

"You look stunning, Krissa," Grace said as she greeted me.

"Thank you."

"Should we finish up?" my dad asked.

"Yes. Just a few, the car will be here shortly," I told him. I was happy to take more pictures, but this time around taking pictures with Braiden felt forced. Usually Braiden would put up with the pictures but tonight he was so detached. I had to place his arms around me for the shots and position us so we at least looked like a couple instead of a brother and sister.

"Car's here," my mom announced.

"All right everybody, let's go," I said as I gathered our belongings. I couldn't help but notice Braiden downing a few extra shots before our exit.

The exit dance was different than any other dance we'd been to. Tonight's dance offered dinner beforehand, allowing the soon to be graduates one last chance to mingle with fellow classmates. We arrived at the hall a little before nine o'clock, entered the grand ballroom located inside our units training facility, and made our way to our table.

The hall was decorated beautifully. Each table was covered in black tablecloths and accented by beautiful floral arrangements with white flowers and silver crystals in large vases with black ribbon tied on the neck of the vase. Each chair had a white cover with a black bow tied around the back. Black, silver and white balloons made a canopy above our heads while the floor to ceiling windows gave an exceptional one hundred and eighty panoramic city view.

"Here's table twelve," I called out to everyone. The six of us took our seats and awaited the arrival of Joy, Gabriel, Charity, and Victor. As our group studied the oversized room with a dance floor in the middle, the other couples joined us at the table.

We passed around compliments, showed off our looks and engaged in trivial conversations while we waited for dinner to begin. The buffet started at nine o'clock, and by ten o'clock the dance floor was filled.

Braiden and I were the last to leave the table to join

everyone. He hadn't said too much to me since we'd arrived, and I was beginning to think the night wasn't going to go as smoothly as I'd planned. "What's wrong?" I asked as we made our way to the outskirts of the wooden floor.

"Nothing. I'm fine."

"You're not acting fine. Are you mad about something?"

"No. I told you I was fine."

"Promise?"

"Yes!" he said, anger flowing through his voice.

I wasn't really sure how to handle this. Should I press the issue or go along with his lies? I didn't want a fight, not tonight, not at the dance. I grabbed his elbow, encouraging our return to the dance floor. Just as he was about to move, he was pushed from behind. I watched as a classmate bumped into Garrett then Garrett into Braiden. I looked at Braiden and saw his once white shirt now soaking wet in red punch.

"I'm so sorry Braiden. I got pushed. Look at your shirt. I'm sorry, man. I'm sure it will come out." Garret was apologizing repeatedly.

"Watch where you're going. My shirt is ruined. What am I supposed to do now?" Everyone noticed the anger radiating from Braiden.

"He didn't mean to. He got pushed," I said, trying to calm him.

"Why are you defending him?"

I wasn't aware I was. "I'm not. Just trying to help."

"Well, it's not working, Krissa. He should have been paying more attention." He glared at Garrett.

"It wasn't his fault." I wasn't trying to defend Garrett, but he wasn't in the wrong.

"Whatever. I'm going to try and wash this off." I followed quickly behind Braiden, looking back to Garrett, hoping he could read my apologetic face.

"Here, let me help you," I told him as I grabbed napkins off the nearest table on our way to the restroom.

"Leave me alone, I'll do it myself!" he snapped as he yanked the linen napkins from my hands. "Why don't you go dance with your man, Garrett," he spat hastily, "after all, he's an option for your pairing right?"

"What? No."

"Really?" He didn't believe me.

"Well, yes, but not really. I have to put three names down, those are the rules. You're my number one. The only chance of me being paired with him is if you don't pick pairing."

"Whatever."

I wasn't sure how to take his words. What did he mean *my man*? Garrett and I had been friends for years now. There was no reason for Braiden to be jealous. I'd introduced him to Garrett way back when we started dating, and there hadn't been any animosity towards him ... until tonight. What had I done to make Braiden lash out, and why was I putting the blame on myself? I couldn't help but let small tears trickle down my cheeks. I felt useless. I didn't know how to make things better, nor did I even know how to stop the uninvited anxiety that was building within me.

As I stood there catching my breath a voice outside my stall door startled me.

"Krissa?"

"Yeah," I answered confused.

"It's Joy." I recognized your shoes. "Are you okay?"

I unlocked the bathroom stall and peeked my head out. "I'm fine, really."

"You don't sound it," she pushed the subject.

"It's Braiden. He's acting so strange tonight. I don't know what's wrong with him."

"Maybe it's the pressure of pairing. I got my sheet today and it's nerve-wracking. I mean, I know where I stand and what I want to do, but still it's so permanent."

"I'm sure Braiden will be fine."

That's what I was always hoping for. That we could just make it work. Deal with the cards we were dealt.

"All right. I'm going to go find Gabriel."

"I'll see you soon."

"There you are!" Honor said as she burst through the bathroom door. "I haven't seen you since dinner."

I kept my head low, avoiding her eyes in the reflection. "Braiden had a drink spilled on him so we've been trying to get the stain out." It wasn't a complete lie, but if that were true, wouldn't I be with him?

"Did it come out?"

"It will. No biggie." I looked up, making the mistake of meeting her eyes.

"Hey, what's wrong? Have you been crying?"

"No, my contact was bugging me. I've been trying to fix it, but it made my makeup run a little."

"I can fix that." She whipped out an eyeliner pen from her clutch and re-applied the liner, erasing all signs of shed tears.

"Thanks," I said, glancing in the mirror. "I better go check on Braiden."

"I'm sure he's fine." She gave a half smile, trying to make me feel better. I knew my best friend well and could see the worry in her eyes.

I found Braiden where I'd left him, impatiently waiting outside the men's bathroom.

"What took you so long?"

"Honor touched up my makeup. I see most of it came out of your shirt."

"I guess."

"It looks good," I said of the faintly pink stained shirt.

"Whatever," he said, avoiding eye contact. "Wait, why was Honor re-doing your makeup?"

"It just started to run a little." I didn't want him to know he'd upset me.

"Tell me you weren't crying?" he said in his condescending

tone.

"No," I lied. I felt foolish for even bringing it up in the first place, but more of a fool for allowing his words to affect me the way they had.

"Good, because there's no reason for you to be upset. You want to dance or something?" he asked, unenthusiastically.

"Okay." What did I do to deserve this?

As the end of the night drew near, I said my good-byes to my friends and unfortunately passed Chance on departure. He pointed his index finger at me as a sly smirk spread across his face. He then pointed his finger upward, displaying the number one. I got his message loud and clear; I was his number one choice. What I didn't understand was why he wasn't getting mine. I met up with Braiden, who was standing alone by the exit, making no attempt to engage with my friends. "You finally ready?" he asked as I approached him.

"Yes, sorry I took so long." Why was I apologizing? It was my night, too. I should've been able to take as long as I wanted without feeling guilty. What had happened to us in the last few days? I'd done everything I could to make him enjoy the night while he did everything he could to spoil it. Was I really going to have to go through the rest of my life feeling so unworthy?

"Joy mentioned something about getting her pairing list, did you get yours?" I tried to make amends.

"Yeah," he answered, avoiding my stare. "Don't worry, you're already printed in my number one spot."

"That doesn't mean you can't choose Single." It was my way of asking what his final decision was.

"I know, Krissa," he let out an irritated sigh. "Do we really have to go there tonight?"

"Our preliminary sheet is due thirty days from graduation, I need to know where you stand."

"Like I said, you're in the number one spot."

That was as good as I was going to get out of him tonight. "Do you still want to come over?"

"I guess so. That was the original plan."

I nodded, feeling no words were necessary. At this point I felt like the sound of my voice was making him cringe. When had I become so irritating to him? And why did I think digging my claws deeper into him wouldn't make me lose my grip on him?

****

We pulled up to my house at midnight, knowing we didn't have too much time considering curfew wasn't far off. "Where's the bottle?" he asked abruptly as we entered the house.

"In my room."

He took off for my bedroom, found the liquor, and took shots straight from the bottle. "Whoa, take it easy. You need to be able to make it into your house."

"I'm fine," he argued as he threw another one back.

In an attempt to save the night, I walked over to him, removed the almost empty bottle from his hand, and wrapped myself in his arms. I wanted to believe that sex could solve all our problems. I shimmied out of my dress and stood in front of him, wearing nothing but a lacey nude bra and matching underwear.

I pushed Braiden off his unbalanced feet on to my bed and climbed on top. "You okay?" I asked, wondering if he was sober enough to function.

"I said I'm fine," he replied as he clumsily reached for me.

I sat atop him but felt so disengaged. He wouldn't even look me in the eye, and while his body moved through the motions, I knew he wasn't with me, mentally or physically. What concerned me the most was that he intentionally drank himself into this stupor.

A relationship that existed so effortlessly only days ago, now seemed to be in ruins. As I looked at Braiden, I realized he was someone I no longer recognized. He was ugly and full of hate. I was sure we were bound for failure. How could we thrive as a couple when we were being forced together?

I didn't know the shell that was lying before me. His body was there, but his soul seemed to have disappeared. I wanted to find him, to bring him back, but when I looked into his eyes they were empty. The perfection I'd desired for so long escaped with no warning. Perfection had evaded us, and I didn't see any intention of it returning.

There wasn't much to say as I drove Braiden home. I wasn't even sure what I wanted to say to the stranger sitting next to me. Deep down I knew it was coming, I saw all the signs. I watched as the train wreck was happening but couldn't step on the brakes. I couldn't turn my back, not now, not this late in the game. Had I wanted to leave, I should've done it many heartbreaks before. I should have walked away several incidents back when he made me feel inadequate, accused me of wrong doing, or just simply made me feel unloved. I made the choice to stick with him because even through all the bad, loving him unconditionally was all that I wanted to do. Even if loving him was ruled by his conditions, I wanted to pair with him; but what if he chose to run?

"I guess I'll see you sometime this week, okay? Call me and let me know when you're free. Good luck with your final." We knew this coming week would be hectic between our finals, graduation, and preparations. Maybe a little time apart would do us good. I wanted to give him space.

"Yup," was all he said as he exited my car and I envisioned him exiting my life.

Sixteen

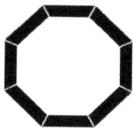

Monday came with little word from Braiden. We talked briefly when I called him, but he complained of all the studying he had to do. Our conversation was ended quickly, providing me no reassurance we were okay.

Tuesday came and went in a similar manner, and again, I looked past his negligence. I finished my last final and expected to feel a huge weight lifted from my shoulders, but that wasn't the case.

During the next couple of days, I tried to get everything in order. I started packing up my room because regardless of where I was placed following graduation, my current home wasn't an option. I emptied my closet and drawers but paused when I noticed the letter from Headquarters on my desk.

I opened the envelope and found my pairing and picking preliminary sheet. I stared at Braiden's name in the number one slot. My heart objected to the next two names I put down, but I wasn't sure what else to do. I needed to put three, I needed to have some sort of back up and decided to put Garrett down in my second slot. He was a good option; I could be comfortable with him, but never fulfilled. Lastly, I put Chance in the number three position. My last two spaces blank. My worst-case scenario was Braiden would choose Single and I'd be left alone, but maybe by some small chance I'd move to Headquarters and find someone better fitted. No. I pushed that thought out of my mind.

With still no word from Braiden, I decided to visit Hope at her job. Her parents owned the dye factory in our unit, and she worked with hopes to one day take over the business. I walked into the large facility through two large steel doors and into the enormous space filled with large, loud machines performing different tasks. I saw products from start to finish as I walked through the maze of machines in search of Hope. I walked to the small back office where I found her sitting at a desk printing out spreadsheets.

"Hey, Krissa, I didn't know you were coming by."

"I was bored and thought I'd kill some time."

"What's Braiden up to?" I knew she was digging for information about us, but I honestly didn't have anything to give.

"Good question. I'm not really sure."

"Is everything all right?" More digging.

"I think so," I answered with a half smile, hoping I looked convincing.

"What's going on Krissa?" Braiden's friend, Owen, asked as he casually walked toward us.

"What are you doing here?" I asked.

"I needed to pick up some fabric for my mom. The Enforcements need new uniforms made for the new hires that will start after picking."

"That's nice of you."

"I guess. Hey, what's the latest with Braiden?"

His question took me off guard. "What do you mean?"

"Oh, nothing," he tried to backtrack as if words slipped by his lips that shouldn't have.

"No, Owen! What's going on?" I don't know why I pushed the issue, but intuition told me something wasn't right.

"Umm …" After a long silence he said, "Look, I think you need to talk to Braiden." He shifted uncomfortably while he stood in the doorway.

Now I was worried. What secret had Owen been let in on? "Where is he?"

"At his house, I think. At least that's where I saw him last."

"You saw him today?" I asked skeptically. I hadn't even been able to get in a conversation with him, but Owen was able to spend the afternoon with him? It was a strange feeling to be jealous of the opposite sex.

"Earlier. I went over to his house for a bit."

"I've got to go. Bye, guys."

"Wait, Krissa, I'll go with you. I get a break, anyway." Hope was quickly on my heels.

"Krissa, please don't say I said anything," Owen pleaded as I made my way to the exit.

I felt like my heart was going to thump out of my chest. Thoughts were racing through my mind that I desperately tried to ignore, but I was entitled to know what was going on. My nervous hand dialed on my communicator and I impatiently waited to hear his voice on the other end.

After a few beeps, we were connected.

"Hey," I said while catching Hope's watchful eyes.

"What's up?" he asked causally, slightly relaxing my nerves.

"Not much. I stopped at the dye factory to see Hope, and I ran into Owen." I tried to match his causal demeanor.

"What's he doing there?"

"Getting some stuff for his parents," I replied. Not letting him change the subject on me, I got back on track. "Well, I hadn't talked to you today, so I thought I'd check in and see what you were up to. Are you doing anything tonight?"

"Nah, I don't think so."

"I could come by, it's still early."

"I should probably stay in tonight." His short answers only added to my frustration.

"Braiden, what's going on?" Hope watched as worry swept over my body as I waited for his response.

"Nothing. Why do you keep asking me that?"

"Because I don't believe you. I know something's wrong."

"Nope."

"Well, even if it wasn't for your short answers and new attitude, Owen already spilled the beans a little." I didn't want to bring him into it, but I needed leverage.

"You talked to Owen?" he asked as his tone of voice softened, sounding sympathetic.

"No, he talked to me."

"Well, what did he say?"

"It's not really about what he said. It was what he wouldn't tell me. He thought it should be coming from you. If you have something to say to me, just say it. It's not fair you involve your friends in matters that pertain to us. I have a right to know what's going on. If it doesn't involve me, I'll drop it. If I do have something to do with it, I would appreciate it if you would clue me in." I didn't mean to sound so angry, but my words were flying out with force.

"Krissa, I'm confused."

"About what?" With no response from him, I asked again, "What are you confused about, Braiden?"

Hope placed her hand on my shoulder when she saw the tears beginning to well in my eyes. I looked up to try and prevent them from running down my cheeks but was unsuccessful. I already knew what his answer was going to be. I'd known it for a while, but I never imagined the intensity of the pain I'd feel when he finally said them.

"I'm not sure if this is what I want anymore. I don't know if I want to be with you."

My ears heard every word, but my head didn't want to register them. I didn't know what to say to him. A million reasons raced through my mind as to why he shouldn't leave me, why he couldn't leave me.

"Look, Krissa ..." His words were backed with a little bit more resentment. This time they weren't as graceful. There was no intention of sparing my feelings. "I don't know if I'm ready for this. I just want to do my own thing and have some freedom. I don't want a pairing. I want to remain a Single."

"You promised me," I said in a low growl full of hurt and anger.

"I don't want this. I need space."

"We were supposed to be paired! What am I supposed to do, Braiden?"

"Krissa, I don't know. I need time to think about things."

"It seems to me you've already made your mind up. Owen knew about your feelings before I did. You must have already had some time to think about it."

"I don't know what I want!"

"You can't expect me to wait around while you figure your shit out."

"I don't expect you to wait around, Krissa."

"We need to talk about this in person. I'm coming over. You don't get to decide this all on your own when it affects both of us."

"You can't come here, Krissa."

"Why not?"

"Because I don't want you here."

"That's bullshit, Braiden! How can you do this to me?" My emotions went from anger to terror and everything in between. One minute I was swearing at him, full of rage, and the next I was begging him.

"I need to see you, Braiden," I repeated myself.

"Fine. Pick me up tomorrow morning for my test. My group is scheduled for eleven o'clock."

"I'll be there at ten o'clock. Please, rethink this Braiden. I'll do whatever it takes."

"Bye." Then there was silence.

"Are you okay? What did he say?"

"I don't understand," I managed to say, as I clung to my device.

"What happened? Krissa?"

"I think Braiden just broke up with me."

"What? Are you serious? Has he lost his mind? Why?"

I couldn't answer her questions. "I don't know. I've got to go."

"Do you want me to drive you home? You aren't looking too good. I've finished all of my work, I'm sure I can leave."

"No, I'll manage. Thank you."

Hope looked at me skeptically, gave me a hug and made her way back to the building. "Call me later."

"Okay."

I got into my car and managed to make it home in my fog of thoughts without wrecking. I walked through my front door, said nothing but 'hellos' to my parents, and crashed on my bed. Even though it was early, I wanted nothing more than to sleep, to escape the awful thoughts racing through my head.

I spent the whole night tossing and turning, trying to get my head right. Dreams gave me no relief, for Braiden monopolized them as well. I woke with dried tears crusted around my eyes, evidence of my pain. I woke only minutes before my alarm went off, leaving me with little time to get ready. I had no appetite so I brushed my teeth, washed my face, and put myself together the best I could and headed to Braiden's house.

I pulled into his driveway at exactly ten o'clock and diverted my attention to the passenger door as he climbed in. "Hey," I said in a calm, steady voice.

"Hi." He sat next to me, avoiding my eyes.

"Are you ready for your final?"

"As ready as I can be."

"I'm sure you'll do fine." After an awkward pause, I put the car in reverse, backed out and headed toward our school. "So, what's going on?"

"I don't know," he said, fidgeting in the seat.

"What do you mean you don't know?"

"I don't know what to do."

"It's pretty simple, Braiden. Our pairing sheet is due. We're supposed to be together."

"Per the enforcements, Krissa. I don't want to be forced into this."

"I don't understand where all of this is coming from. Did I do something? We were fine days ago and now all of a sudden you want to throw in the towel. What gives?"

"You didn't do anything. It's not you, it's me."

Was he really using *that* line? That was his logic? No shit, it was all him. "You're going to have to do better than that. That isn't good enough. After all we've been through, I deserve a better explanation than that."

"It's hard to explain." He redirected his attention out the passenger window.

"Try," I said angrily.

"We don't feel right anymore. It's just not working."

"You don't love me anymore?"

"Krissa, I don't even know what love is."

Those words took my breath away. How could he not know what love was? What had we been doing for the past months? He never loved me? My stomach knotted and the urge to throw up was suddenly present. We'd gone round for round, and I kept up the fight until I heard those words. Now there was no need for him to throw in the towel, I was done. His words knocked me out.

I pulled into the furthest parking spot from the school in hopes of prolonging our conversation, eventhough I didn't know what to say.

"I've got to go."

I sat in silence.

"All right, I'll see you around. I'm sorry Krissa."

"This is what you really want? You're just going to give up? Just let me go? You won't even fight for me?"

"Pairing isn't worth fighting for. I'm sorry."

His apology meant nothing.

As I made my way to the main road, instead of taking my normal left to go home, I took a right needing to get away. I didn't know where I was going, I just wanted to escape albeit I knew there was really no way out of here, both figuratively and literally.

While I tried to put on a brave front when I finally made it home, my mom saw through my disguise. She could read past what I was saying to see what I was feeling. I tried to be strong and tell her I was fine, but she knew better.

"He wants freedom, to remain a Single. I don't know where that leaves me. We're supposed to be paired, but he doesn't want me."

"I can't believe he did that to you, Krissa. After all you've been through, how could he just turn his back on you? If that's how he really feels, you don't need him in your life. You deserve someone so much better. It'll work out, honey. Now you'll live out the life you've always dreamt of. The enforcements know what they're doing," she reassured me. A part of me felt it would work because I'd always trusted in the system, but a part of me worried it wouldn't be what I wanted.

I could tell her heart was breaking from the pain I was in, but past that I sensed excitement. I had nothing keeping me from my dreams. I'd be able to move to the Headquarters and live the life

I'd always thought I'd have. A part of me wanted to see things her way, but I just couldn't.

Seventeen

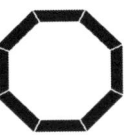

Knock. Knock. "Good morning, Krissa. Happy Graduation Day!"

I rolled over to face my door. "Eh, good morning, Mom." She walked over with a large glass overflowing with champagne and fresh strawberries. "Geez, are you trying to get me drunk before the ceremony?"

"No. Just something special for your special day. You've got to get ready."

I tried to act excited about my graduation, but a black cloud hung over me. I wanted to be excited about moving on in my life, but how could I do that when I was stuck in the past?

"Everybody is on their way. Your grandparents will meet us at the school, and the rest of the family will be here when we get back. Hurry up and get ready. We've got to leave in thirty minutes."

"Okay, I'll be ready." I popped a champagne flavored strawberry in my mouth. Maybe a little alcohol would be good for me, numb the pain a little.

I didn't do much to get ready. I put on little makeup, just to disguise my sleepless eyes, I wore my hair down and straight, topped with a cardboard square on my head, and I was wearing a polyester sunshine yellow gown with our units emblem embroidered on the left arm. There was nothing I could've done to enhance the fashion disaster that stood in my reflection.

"Oh, sweetie, I'm so proud of you. I can't say it enough," my mom told me as we walked into my high school.

"I know, Mom, thanks."

"We're going to go find our seats. Your grandparents are already here."

"See you out there." I walked away toward my classmates who were beginning to form the processional line.

"All right everyone, find your places," Principal Maxx began. "It'll be just how we practiced. Congratulations everyone for making it here. It's been a pleasure spending the last four years with you fine young people." Yadda, Yadda, Yadda. He was supposed to say that stuff, right?

I scanned the line for Braiden, finding the back of his head immediately brought butterflies with enormous wings to my stomach. I was filled with excitement and angst, and while I was near him, I was nowhere near close to his heart.

The music began and our class proceeded down the auditorium aisles and to the stage. When I saw my family, I felt guilty. I was supported by the most loving family while I so selfishly continued to worry over Braiden and what my future would look like without him.

It'd been a couple of days since I left him in the school parking lot, and although we hadn't spoken since, I held out a tiny bit of hope that he'd come to his senses. I was so consumed by my thoughts about Braiden, I didn't hear my name being called to accept my graduation certificate.

"Krissa, that's you," Hope said tapping me on the shoulder. I got out of my seat, glanced to the row behind me and mouthed *thank you* to her. It was official, I was a graduate. Yippee. I should've been on the same high as the rest of my friends, but I wasn't.

"Let me see it," my dad said of my certificate. "Wow. My little girl is all grown up." He stared at the sheet of paper between his hands that was covered with thin plastic and backed with cardboard.

"Krissa, we're so proud of you. Our first grandchild, graduating! Now we wait and see where you're placed. Are your lists ready?" my grandmother asked.

"Pretty much," I lied.

"Hopefully you'll end up at Headquarters," my mom stated. "But I wouldn't be disappointed if you stayed here."

"Time will tell."

I didn't know where I belonged. My heart wanted to be with Braiden, but if he didn't allow that then I needed to be far, far away from him. Headquarters was listed as my first choice, then my current unit and lastly my mom's family's unit. Waiting to hear about my future would be torture. I was supposed to be paired with Braiden, living in Headquarters, but I ventured that was very unlikely.

"We did it. Finally!" Honor exclaimed as she darted toward me.

"I know," I said as we wrapped our arms around one another. "Hey Dad, can you take a picture of us?"

"Sure, sweetie."

Honor and I posed and flashed our pearly whites. "Cheese!" we said simultaneously.

"We've got to get going. I've got to finish setting up for the party. I'll see you soon." I gave Honor a quick hug then rushed off.

I was eager to see the rest of my family and party with my friends, but I couldn't shake the thought that Braiden may not show.

An hour later I stood in my backyard taking in the abundance of decorations. I focused my attention on two large frames setting on a table near several gifts.

"I'm sorry," Mom said as she crept up behind me and hugged me.

"It's all right." I stared at the collage of pictures.

I stared at the first frame with all of the pictures from my senior dances. "It's fine, really. I love them. You did a great job." I scanned the photos of Braiden and I dressed up, posing for the camera. The largest picture, my favorite of us, was taken at the year-end dance. My stomach burned with pain. I was staring at the happiest night I'd spent with him.

I walked to the other end of the tent and stood in front of the other frame. I smiled, putting on a brave face. The pictures ran left to right in the sequence of my life. The frame represented my life, my family, and my friends but I couldn't focus on anything but the last picture, again of Braiden and me. This picture was from when we celebrated Christmas with my dad's family, the night I conceived. As I lost myself in the memory, a flood of emotions washed over me. Not only did it remind me of Braiden, but also the baby I lost along the way. Just when I started healing and seeing the positives, the scab was ripped off, the wound reopened. I tried to remain calm on the outside; not giving away any hint to the storm that was raging inside me.

"Are you okay?" my mom asked hesitantly.

"I'm good." I kept a bold face until I went into my bathroom. I shut and locked the door and finally allowed my feelings to surface.

I emerged from the bathroom five minutes later, my face put back together and my emotions in check. Nobody needed to see my torment, this was my battle. I didn't need anyone fighting it along side of me. I buried my thoughts deep in the back of my brain, hiding them.

"Hey Kris."

"Hey girl," I said to Honor.

"What can I do to help?" she asked eagerly.

"Mom," I yelled into the house, "what do you want Honor

and me to do?"

"How about you girls get the food together?"

"Okay."

As busy as I kept myself, I couldn't help but wonder if Braiden would grace us with his presence.

Within the hour, our house and yard were filled with family and friends. I opened presents, cut my cake and chatted with everyone who came to celebrate. Everyone except Braiden. I was grateful for everyone, especially my parents for all they'd done for me, but I was distracted by Braiden's absence. I snuck away for a few moments during the party to call him, but Grace informed me he was out for the night.

"There you are," Honor said as she found me out front walking back up my driveway, communicator in hand with disappointment written across my face.

"Hey," I said, adding a fake smile.

"What's going on?"

"Nothing, I'm fine."

"Want to talk about it?"

"Not really."

"Don't let it bother you, Kris. You deserve so much better. He's better off with her, anyway."

I was half listening when I realized she was talking about something I wasn't expecting to hear. "Better off with whom?" I asked as my heart rate accelerated.

Her face turned red as she asked, "Weren't you just talking to

Braiden? Didn't he tell you? Isn't that why you're upset?"

"Tell me what?"

"Nothing. I shouldn't have said anything," she said, biting her fingernails.

"Yes you should have! You're my best friend. What aren't you telling me?"

I could see her trying to figure out the best way to approach it. "I just got off the phone with Emery. He's at Owen's party and he saw Braiden there."

"And?"

"He was there with Harmony."

"What?" I heard her loud and clear, I was just in disbelief.

"Emery isn't sure what happened. One minute they were on the couch and the next he saw them walking upstairs. I'm really sorry. You are so much better than that, better off without him. He doesn't deserve you."

Yes he does, I thought. I just don't deserve this pain. I don't care if he's worthy of me or not, I'd give anything to have him back. If it's true and he doesn't deserve me, shouldn't I be the one making the decisions?

"Krissa? Are you okay? Say something."

"Do you think they ..."

"No!" she said abruptly, but her expression didn't match the certainty in her voice.

"I need to talk to him."

"You need to forget about him. Come back and enjoy your

party. Please. I'm sorry I said anything. I didn't mean to ruin your day."

She draped her arm around my shoulders and led the way back to my party.

Eighteen

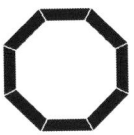

My family left the following day leaving me with a lot of time on my hands and nothing to fill it. I knew I shouldn't want to see Braiden, but I needed answers.

I decided to drive to Braiden's house.

I knocked on his front door while my heart thumped every bit as hard against my chest. Just needing to see him, I didn't know what I was going to say to him, I hadn't thought that far ahead.

"Hey," I said nervously as he opened the glass storm door.

"Hey," he looked confused, "what are you doing here?" He stepped on to the front porch; it was obvious he wasn't going to invite me in.

"I figured I'd have more success showing up than trying to get you on your communicator.

"I was busy," he told me without daring to look me in the face.

"Doing what? Or should I say, *who*?"

He whipped his head toward me as the color in his face drained. "What are you talking about, Krissa?"

That got his attention. "You know what I'm talking about." I wasn't sure where I mustered up the courage to have this conversation, but I wasn't going to back down. I stared him in the eye. "Emery saw you, he told Honor and of course she told me. How could you?"

"It's not like that."

"Oh really? Then what's it like? Please, feel free to elaborate."

"Nothing happened." His features were hard as stone, but his eyes were weak.

"Really?" I asked, not believing a word he was telling me. "So, what? You were just giving her a tour of the upstairs bedrooms?"

"We're not together anymore, Krissa."

"So that gives you free rein to fuck every girl you come in contact with, with no consideration for me?"

"I didn't sleep with her."

I rolled my eyes and gave him that *yeah right* look.

"I didn't! I just kissed her."

I continued to scowl.

"We hooked up. Nothing serious. I didn't have sex with her." He crossed his arms, putting up more of a wall between us.

"That's so much better. Very comforting."

"I was drunk."

"That's not an excuse!" My stomach was turning. "What if the situation was reversed, Braiden? What if I was at a party and I hooked up with someone? Put yourself in my shoes. How would you feel?"

"I don't owe you anything. We aren't together."

"We're supposed to be."

"Only if I let the government force me into it."

He was right, but I never thought he'd see it that way. He was right, he didn't owe me anything, but honestly, I expected a much higher degree of respect. "When I asked you if you were breaking up with me to be with other people you said no. You were lying."

"No. I didn't plan on it. It just happened."

"So it's okay for you, but not for me? I really love your double standards." My sarcasm wasn't missed.

"You're free to do whatever you want. If that's what you want to do, then go for it," he said as he used his hand to shoo me off.

He didn't love me and didn't want to learn how, and I needed to accept that. I turned around without saying a word. He was no longer mine.

I needed to get away and clear my head a little. While I didn't really feel like it, I decided to head downtown and do some window shopping for my new place. I was desperate for any kind of distraction. I entered through the doors of the home furnishing store and was looking at nothing in particular when I looked up and locked eyes with Chance. I gave him a small wave and half expected him to keep walking, but I should have known better.

"Hey Kris," he said as he approached me. "I saw you through the window and thought I'd come in and say hi. How are you?" he asked, leaning against the display. I hadn't spoken to Chance since our run in at the dance. I knew his question was deeper than just casual conversation.

"I'm good," I said, remembering to add a smile.

"You sure? I heard what happened, and I'm really sorry."

"Yes, I'm sure."

"You don't have to pretend Kris. I know you. I know you're not all right."

"Chance, don't. Please. I don't want to talk about it, especially here."

"Well, then let's get away from here. What are you doing later? "

"Umm, nothing really. No plans." *Great. Nicely done, Krissa,* my logic mocked me.

"Do you want to hang out?"

No! Say no. "Sure." I wondered if I was going to say the opposite of everything I was thinking for the rest of the night. It felt like my mouth and brain were at war. "Just as friends, right?" I blurted. My brain and lips were finally trying to get along.

"Just as friends."

"I'm free around nine o'clock."

"Meet me at my house then?"

"All right, see you then." He waved good-bye and exited the store.

I could handle this. In many ways I missed having Chance around.

After a bit of self-doubt, I got into my car and made my way down the familiar road to Chance's house. I pulled into his driveway at 9:35. By the time I was out of my car, Chance was waiting for me outside his front door.

"You made it," he said with excitement.

"I did. So what do you want to do?"

"Are you hungry?'

I was never hungry anymore. "Sure."

"What do you feel like?"

"Whatever, your choice." I followed him into the standard sized home for a family of four.

"How about pizza? Nina's can deliver," he said, grabbing his communicator.

"Sounds good."

Chance placed our order for pizza then suggested we go outside on the old wooden loveseat swing, my favorite place to hang when we were together. We made our way downstairs and outside to the garden that his mom had worked so diligently on.

"I'm glad you came over," Chance said as he took the seat next to me.

"Me too. It's nice to be able to just hang out with you without getting the third degree about it."

"What do you mean?'

"Braiden always hated when I did anything that included you, even fitness class."

"That's ridiculous."

"That was without him knowing your attempts to win me back."

"Thanks for not telling him."

"I didn't do it for you."

"I know. He wasn't nice to you Kris. He changed you and not for the better."

"Gee, thanks, Chance."

"I didn't mean it like that. I'm glad you're not together anymore. Do I want you back? Yeah. Are my chances better now? I hope so, but I miss the old Krissa." He reached for my hand, and I didn't pull it out from under his.

"I didn't change that much." I avoided the other points he made.

"Yes, you did. You lost your spark. You lost your confidence. You were so outgoing before, so energetic. He drained you."

The only thing he drained from me was my life when he left. He sucked my existence right out. I'm changed now, now that he's gone.

Thankfully the pizza delivery guy interrupted our intense conversation. I wasn't really sure how to respond to Chance's accusations. I needed a break. It was nice to know Chance was on my side, but it didn't lessen my pain. Throughout my relationship with Braiden, everyone kept reminding me how different I'd become. Sure, I'd changed a little, but I didn't think it was that drastically. I thought it was for the better. I was tamer, maybe a little less righteous, a little less flirtatious. I felt different now that

Braiden had ditched me for good. My smile wasn't bright anymore. Hell, it wasn't even real. I wanted to double over in pain. My heart physically hurt; I was definitely worse now.

We sat in his living room eating pepperoni pizza when it dawned on me we were the only ones in his house. "Your house is quiet tonight, where is everyone?"

"Mom and Dad are out with some friends for the evening."

"Smooth, Chance. I'll give you that much. You definitely know how to work it. Where's your girlfriend?"

"We broke up." I knew that already, heard it a few weeks after the year-end dance, but I wanted confirmation. I certainly didn't need any more drama because I knew what it felt like to have someone creep in on what you thought was yours. I didn't want to be that girl.

"I'm sorry to hear that." And I was. Breakups were never easy. There's really no such thing as a mutual split.

"I'm not. She wasn't you, Kris. I told you I wasn't going to give up," he said, taking our empty plates and setting them on the table. He moved closer to me on the couch, closing the one cushion space that was between us. "We broke up because you were my number one. She found out and freaked. She was on my list, but she wasn't my first choice."

"There's still a chance you'll be paired. You should work it out with her."

"It's a risk I'm willing to take. I want you."

I was too weak to fight him off. I was sick of fighting. Fighting to win Braiden back. Fighting off Chance.

"Chance, I'm not ready. Honestly, I'm too broken. I can't do--"

Mid-sentence he grabbed my face with both hands and drew it to his. He slipped his tongue past my lips and found mine.

However, it was all wrong! His lips were bigger. His mouth was more aggressive. The taste was different. It wasn't right. It wasn't what I'd grown accustomed to. It was sloppy and messy. Our heads were going the same direction and we were snagging lips and tongues with our teeth. For a couple that meshed well a year ago, we were so disconnected now. Chance was a stranger to me. I was accustomed to someone else and the person in front of me wasn't what I knew. He wasn't what I wanted.

I did nothing to stop him as we worked our way from the couch to the floor, my shirt unbuttoned, and my skirt around my waist, and he was in me.

"I've missed you," he said through a moan.

I stared up at him, flashed another fake smile and pulled him closer to me. I clutched him tighter, hiding my face, hiding my lies. I didn't feel the same for him. I hadn't missed him, and I wasn't sure why I was there. He was my safety net even though I really didn't want him to be. He was saying everything I wanted to hear, the voice was just wrong. Accepting his words because I wanted to hear them, I just closed my eyes and pictured Braiden instead.

"I love you, Kris. I never stopped." His motions slowed and he lay on top of me, catching his breath.

"You've changed. Where was this Chance a year ago?"

"It just took me some time to grow up. To realize what I was missing." Either he really had changed or his acting skills were unprecedented. "Are you okay?" he asked, gathering his pile of clothes from the floor.

"I'm fine."

"You sure?"

"Yes."

"Just wanted to make sure. I know this is a lot to take in. Krissa, will you please consider putting me in your top spot. I will do anything you want. We could be great together. Can't you see that?"

"I need time to think about things Chance. Let's take things slow."

"Our sheets are due this week. I've already told you what I'm doing, and I think you know what you should do. Think about it okay?"

"Okay." I knew Braiden wasn't a good fit for me, but I loved him still. However, if he removed himself, what other option did he leave me with?

"Do you want to watch something?" he asked as I finished putting myself back together.

"Sure, for a little bit. I need to be home before curfew."

"You can't stay?"

Technically, yes I could have, but I didn't think that was in either of our best interests for me to stay. "Not tonight. Let's quit while we're ahead." Maybe he was ahead, but I sure as shit wasn't. I was way behind, watching it all unravel.

I left his house at one a.m. after a long embrace filled with kisses, and I drove down the empty streets in a blur. My encounter with Chance flooded my brain, leaving me more uncertain than ever. I defended my actions by reminding myself this was what Braiden wanted, what he'd pushed for. Probably not this exact situation, but ultimately the decision was his. He deserved this. Did Chance? Had I just used him? I certainly didn't want what had happened, but I allowed it. I wanted to hurt Braiden the way that he'd hurt me, but I didn't mean for Chance to get in the way.

I had a history with Chance, which made my actions so easy with Chance. There were feelings for Chance, they were old and dusty, but they could make a comeback. I could revert to my old self. I could settle, I guess. I mean, I'd been down that road before and was happy; couldn't I bring myself to that place again?

Tonight was the first night I felt like I was in control again. I knew Braiden would be angry, but I also knew it would disgust him. I finally gave him a reason to not want to be with me. He left me for no reason, and that I couldn't accept. Now I gave him a reason to reject me.

Nineteen

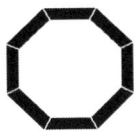

I woke up to the sound of my communicator going off at 11:30 the next morning. I'd finally slept through the night. There was still pain but no anxiety. I felt at peace.

"Hello?" I asked in my raspy morning voice.

"Krissa, it's Braiden."

I didn't know what to say. I was taken off guard by his unexpected call.

"You there?"

"I'm here."

"How are you?"

"Fine." Weird. What did he care?

"Listen, I need to see you. We need to talk."

"I'm done talking. There's nothing left to say. I told you my fight was over. You won." Wow, did I really just say that? I was so accustomed to not saying anything that would upset him or push him away. But not this time. This time I had no filter.

"Please, Krissa. I messed up. I'm sorry. I ... I want you back."

If only he had said this yesterday. "No you don't, at least you won't. We have a lot to talk about."

"What are you talking about?'

I decided I'd go to Braiden's so I put together a knockout look. I wanted him to see me in this light. I wasn't proud of what I'd done the night before, but it boosted my confidence. I was no longer drowning, just treading water. He'd broken me, but I'd managed to glue myself back together.

****

"So," I sat two steps below him, "what's this all about?" I was determined to stay focused.

"I was stupid," he said apologetically.

"You realized that in a matter of three days?"

"Yes. I made a mistake." He looked like hell; clearly sleep had evaded him in the last couple of days.

"There's a lot you need to know, Braiden."

"So it's true?"

He caught me off guard with his question. "Is what true?"

"You and Chance?"

"What did you hear?"

"Chance told Pax and Tobin everything this morning."

"It's true." There was no reason to hold back.

"You've got to be kidding me." He stood up in fury pacing back in forth in front of me. "How could you?"

"We're not together anymore, Braiden. I'm free, right? This is what you wanted!" I moved closer. "I would've been with you forever. Chance was never an issue, would've never been an issue, but you walked away. You left me! He was telling me everything I wanted to hear from you, but you were telling me the opposite. You broke me, so I tried to let him fix me."

"Do you want to be with him? Is he your number one?"

"You are, but if I can't have you, I don't know what else to do." I didn't necessarily want to be with Chance, but it was better than being alone, better than sitting around thinking about what I'd had with Braiden.

"We can get over this."

"What?"

"I can get over it, Krissa. We can do this." He slid his arms around my hips.

"You're going to pick me? You're going to be paired?" I asked skeptically. "You want me back after I slept with Chance?" I pulled my upper body away from him, but not enough to escape his embrace.

"He's not my best friend anymore, but yes. He doesn't get to have you."

"Why now? Because someone else wanted me?"

"No." I thought for a moment I saw the lie. "I don't want to be without you." His words taunted me. I saw a glimpse of the future we could have and chose to ignore the hurt he could potentially bring.

"I want this to work, Braiden, but I'm scared you're going to hurt me."

"I won't."

My head said no, but my heart made me stay. They never seemed to work on the same frequency anymore. "Okay."

"Really?" he said enthusiastically.

"Yes, but I need to talk to Chance."

"You can't. You're not going to see him."

"Yes, I can. I need to. I owe him that."

"You don't owe him anything."

"Listen, he may have hurt you, but he was kind to me. He was there when you weren't."

"Fine, Krissa, do what you want."

"It's about what's right."

He finally agreed, but he wasn't happy about it. When deciding to take him back, I also decided I wasn't going to let him dictate my life anymore. I had every intention of not allowing him to control me.

****

I already regretted the conversation I was about to have with Chance, but I owed him an explanation. I knew most people would feel as if it was karma for the way he treated me, but what I was about to do wasn't fair. He didn't necessarily deserve better, but I hated to be the one breaking his heart. I cared about Chance; I just cared more about Braiden.

I parked in the driveway and walked up the narrow path and knocked. Deep down I wished no one would answer.

"I was just about to call you." I wouldn't have believed the old Chance, but something in the way he said it made me a believer.

"Hi." I knew I had guilt written across my face.

"How are you?" he asked, pulling me in for a hug and kiss. Our lips met uncomfortably and I knew he felt my resistance. "What's wrong?"

"Braiden found out about us from Tobin and Pax."

"Are you mad?"

"It complicates things for me."

"Braiden can just get over it," he said, sounding victorious.

"It's not as simple as that," I said, biting my lower lip.

"Don't worry about him, Kris."

"Chance, he wants me back."

"You're going to go back to him, aren't you?"

"I have to."

"No, you don't. You have a choice."

"I don't have a choice." Which was true in every sense of the phrase. "I have to go back. I love him."

"And you don't love me?"

"Not like that. I know it's not fair."

"So, last night meant nothing?" He slammed his fist into the doorframe.

No amount of apologizing would make up for my inexcusable actions.

"You're just going to let him in like that?" He snapped his fingers. "He doesn't deserve you. He's going to hurt you."

"It's a risk I'm willing to take." I had no option but to take it.

"It's not worth it."

"You have time to change your list. I don't need to be your number one." I grabbed his swelling hand.

"That's not for you to worry about." He retracted his hand.

He slammed the door in my face and a part of my heart mourned for him. I also knew that a huge part of my heart, a more important part, wouldn't feel sorrow anymore. I no longer felt the loss of my true love. I knew my reasons for loving Braiden weren't just, but I loved him irrationally. Whether he deserved it or not didn't matter because either way Headquarters forced me to shower him with it.

Twenty

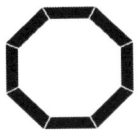

Everyone could see the change in me over the next few weeks. I was happy, but I could tell my friends weren't particularly in favor of our rekindling ... least supportive was my mother.

"What are your plans for today?" my mom asked as we sat down for lunch at Nina's.

"I think Braiden and I are going to hang out for a little bit. I need to give him his gift."

"I still can't believe you went through all that trouble," she said, taking a sip of her tea.

"It wasn't too difficult."

"It wasn't easy."

She was right. I had to search high and low to find a map of our country pre-World War III. He had an obsession of what our land used to look like, and I knew he desperately wanted one.

"Does he deserve it? Look at what he's put you through, Krissa." I was well aware of everything he'd put me through, but I was willing to let him make up for it.

"I know, Mom, but I'm the one that had to deal with it, not

you. I think he's worth it."

"I had to see you through it and hate him for it. I wish you had another option. I don't want you paired with him. It's like they're making you settle. He should've remained a Single and get moved to the Sweeper unit."

"Don't say that! I'm not settling, Mom. I love him." I buried my face into the menu.

"Does he love you?"

I let out a sigh because I wasn't sure of the answer. "It'll be fine, Mom, really. You've got to let go and have faith."

"I just don't want him to hurt you again. I'll kill him if he does."

"He won't."

"I hope not," she said, finally ending our discussion on Braiden.

We parted ways after lunch, and I picked up Braiden a short time later.

"Hey!" I almost screeched in excitement when he got into my car.

"Hi," he said, less enthusiastic than I'd been.

"You ready? I have lots of fun stuff planned."

"Yup."

"Your parents know you won't be coming home tonight, right?"

"Yeah, I told them I was staying at Tobin's."

"Perfect!"

"So what's the plan?"

"Dinner. Your choice, my treat."

"Something quick and easy. Like you," he slipped in. Ouch. That was a hit below the belt.

"What?" I was disgusted by the comment.

He snickered, "Just kidding. I'm just messing with you."

"It wasn't funny. Why would you say that?"

"Isn't it true?" I guess it was but I thought we were moving past our past. I was sorry for what I'd done but that didn't give Braiden the right to hang that over my head.

"What do you want for dinner?" I ignored his hurtful words.

After another meal at Nina's, we continued our date at the upscale hotel downtown. I opened the door to the king sized suite and walked across the plush carpet, opening a bottle of liquor I'd brought to help celebrate. After pouring us each a shot, I handed a glass to Braiden and lifted my own in toast.

"Cheers." We raised our shot glasses and clinked them together. The liquid burned but took the edge off. A few drinks later and we both felt really good. I didn't care that I needed to intoxicate my boyfriend, I was just glad his sour attitude had been lost.

"Here you go. I hope you like it." I handed him a gift bag.

He took the handles from me tore out the tissue paper took one look at the gift and his mouth dropped open.

"Do you like it?"

"It's perfect. How'd you get this?"

"I'll never tell," I joked with him

"Thank you. It's exactly what I needed."

"I'm going to go to the bathroom, I'll be right out."

"Okay. I'll be waiting right here."

Once inside the bathroom, I slipped on a black sheer bra and matching panties then clasped the black lacy garter to my black thigh-highs.

I emerged and stood before him, "What do you think?" I spun around to show off my outfit.

"Sexy," he managed to stutter.

This time around, he wasn't angry, but he was just as distant. There was plenty of sexual chemistry, but there was nothing behind it. His kisses felt right, I knew his familiar lips, his touch was what I'd longed for, but there was no substance.

I rolled off of him after our sweaty workout and gathered my bra and panties off the floor. I wanted to be able to clean up our relationship like I'd cleaned up the room; pick up the pieces and put them where they belong. I didn't want the mess.

I stood in front of the ceramic sink and stared at my reflection. I didn't want to believe the person I was staring at was me. I looked worn out, unhappy even though Braiden was in my life, what life did I really have?

I emerged from the bathroom minutes later to find Braiden passed out on the luxurious bed. I crept to the other side and climbed in. I rolled over to my left side while grabbing Braiden's right arm to cuddle. I snuggled close to him and listened to his heartbeat.

"I love you," I whispered. Maybe it was the alcohol, maybe it was sleep deprivation, but after my words were said, he retracted his arm, turned away from me and went to sleep with no response.

This is what my future held.

I wasn't asleep long before the vibrations of my communicator woke me. I answered it without looking at the caller identification.

"Hello?"

"Kris. It's me."

"What are you doing calling me? Are you okay? What's going on?" I was confused.

"I'm outside."

"Outside?"

"Of your hotel room."

"What? What are you doing here?"

"Come out."

"You're going to get into trouble. You're breaking curfew."

"I don't care, it's worth the risk."

"I can't. I'm here with Braiden. I'm not coming out."

"Please, Kris. I'm taking a big chance here. Hear me out?" I contemplated and decided to give in. I had a feeling his persistence wouldn't fade. I looked over at Braiden sleeping as far away from me as possible, realizing he was out like a rock.

"Braiden?" I whispered, making sure he was sleeping soundly.

No response. I crept out of the bed hoping he wouldn't stir. I threw on more appropriate clothing and headed for the door.

I opened the door and came face to face with Chance.

"What the hell are you doing here?" I hissed, dragging him down the hall.

His eyes scanned my body and I knew he wanted to comment on my thin tank and too short shorts.

"Kris, are you crazy? Have you gone mad? I'm serious. What are you doing with him?" He pointed down the hall. "I know you told me you were going to work things out with him, but by now you must have realized that was a mistake."

"Chance! We've been over this."

"I'm better for you." He placed his hand on my shoulder.

"I'm sorry. I can't. I'm sorry for what we did and for what I'm putting you through now."

"You regret me?" he asked, staring me dead in the eyes.

"I was in a really bad place, and I made a bad choice. I'm sorry I hurt you."

"What about *your* pain, Kris?"

"I don't have pain." I dropped the eye contact.

"Bullshit. I know you better than that. I can see your pain. It's written all over your face."

"You need to accept what I'm telling you."

"No. I won't accept it!"

"Chance, ahhh." I was so frustrated, so ... torn. "There are so many reasons as to why we can't be. I love Braiden. I want

Braiden in my life. There is more to it, it's complicated."

"Let me make things easy for you."

"You can't! I'm automatically paired with Braiden." In a way it slipped out; in a way I wanted him to know.

"That can't be."

"It is. I don't have a choice."

"How is it possible?"

"Chance I don't want to go there with you. Can't you just accept it and leave well enough alone?"

"No. I want to hear it all."

"Fine! Earlier this year I got pregnant. I lost the baby but was automatically paired with Braiden." The secret I'd tried so desperately to hide, to run from, was now out in the open. My truths were laid out on the table for him to see.

"Say something, please."

"I have to go," he said with fury as he pushed past me toward the elevator.

I was left alone in the hallway, adrenaline pulsing through my body, worry and relief fighting to make their presence known.

I made my way back into our room, making as little noise as possible. I shut the door and flipped the dead bolt. The click of the lock startled Braiden, waking him into disorientation.

"What are you doing?" he asked, confused.

I should've told him but I didn't want to upset him. I'd done enough of that already. I knew he wouldn't understand, nor did I think he would've believed me if I told him the truth. "I heard a noise out in the hall. I went out to see what it was."

"You woke me up," he stated annoyed, whipping his head back down on the pillow.

"Sorry." I tiptoed back to my spot on the bed. "Good night." My life with Braiden was full of apologies.

"Ahh," he let out a disgruntled sigh. "Night." He faced the wall.

****

Sleep never came to me. "Good morning." He was finally awake.

"Morning."

"Did you sleep okay?" I pulled myself upright, dangling my feet off the bed.

"Good enough I guess."

"I didn't mean to wake you."

"Whatever." He rubbed his face with the palms of his hands.

"Do you want to go grab some lunch or something?"

"Actually, I told the guys I'd hang out with them today."

"Oh." I knew he could sense my disappointment, but it didn't seem to affect him any.

"I think I'll just head home."

"Thanks for spending your birthday with me. I hope you enjoyed it."

"I did. Thanks for my gift."

"You're welcome. Give me a call sometime later this week. I don't have much going on."

"I do. I'm leaving with Leon to visit his family for a couple of days."

"When you get back then?"

"Sure. I'm going to head out."

"Do you want a ride? I can take you home."

"No, I'm good. I'll talk to you later." I watched him head off, finding it hard to believe we were back in a relationship.

Twenty One

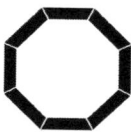

"So you've turned in your sheet?"

Absolutely, it was due a week ago. "Of course." We sat down at the last booth inside Nina's and started eating our pizza. "You put Emery down as your number one, right?"

"Yes, but it really doesn't matter considering I'll have another year to wait. I'm going to start my training here. I'm assuming you chose Braiden as your number one?" Honor accused more than questioned.

"Yes, and I chose Headquarters."

"That part I'm okay with."

"But not my picking?"

"Kris, you went through hell with him."

"It wasn't that bad."

"It was, and I hope by some miracle you'll meet someone at Headquarters who'll change your choice. I believe in this upcoming year you'll see that your pick needs to change."

"Don't hold your breath." I appreciated her concern for me,

but I was content with my pairing.

During our conversation I couldn't help but notice two Headquarters Enforcers enter the restaurant. Dressed in black, aside from the Headquarters' logo, and armed with guns, they looked intimidating.

"I wonder what's going on. We weren't informed of a visit." Honor stared at the officers speaking with the restaurant manager.

"I don't know."

"Do you think someone's in trouble?"

"Who knows." I tried to sound casual, but the anxiety could be heard in my voice, especially when their stares focused on me.

"Krissa Channing?"

I nervously looked up at the two muscular men standing over us. "Yes?" I tried to steady my voice.

"Could you please follow us?"

"Sure. May I ask what this is about?"

"Follow us, please." I wasn't about to argue.

"Can I come?"

"No, ma'am, we only need Miss Channing."

Panic washed over me. "Its fine, Honor, I'm sure it's nothing." I flashed my biggest smile, not sure if I was trying to convince her or myself.

As we exited the restaurant, we hung a right and proceeded to walk downtown. Watchful eyes were cast in our direction, speculating as we passed, but no one actually knew why I was being escorted.

"Where are we going?"

"This way, please." After a short walk, we entered the City Center's back entrance.

"Am I in trouble? Is my family all right?"

"We'll answer all of your questions in just a bit." They led me down a small corridor and into a small rectangular room that looked like an interrogation room. I took a seat at the sole table while the men sat across from me.

"Let's get started," the man to the left stated. "We received your pairing paperwork. Given the circumstances between you and Braiden Connor regarding the pregnancy, it was automatically decided that the two of you would be paired. We know that you picked the Headquarters as your number one location, however after reviewing Mr. Connor's paperwork, we seem to have run into a problem.

"Okay. What is the problem?" I asked skeptically.

"Krissa, his pairing and picking sheet was left blank."

"Blank?" I questioned.

"Yes, he didn't put anywhere or anyone down."

This whole time he'd been playing me. "There must be some kind of mistake." That had to be it. He wouldn't do that to me, would he?

"You're saying you didn't know anything about this?"

"Of course not." Up until a minute ago I saw my future at the Headquarters with Braiden. I wish I had known. "Can I talk to him?

Where is he?" I was ready to tear him apart.

"Krissa, there's more to it. He left a note on his sheet explaining where we'd find his communicator, which had more information."

"What?"

"Here." They pulled down a screen that was attached to the wall and plugged in a communicator. I watched in disbelief as Braiden appeared on the screen in front of me.

I've turned in my communicator, hoping to relinquish your right of getting in touch with me or tracking me. I no longer want to be subjected to the Headquarter's control and I've found a way out.

Krissa, I'm hoping you'll see this and understand. Our relationship was full of mistakes. From start to finish and everything in between, it was a mistake and I'm sorry for everything I've put you through and everything you're about to go through. I can't do it. I knew I never could. I won't be paired. I won't live by their rules. I have no direction, no plan aside from the fact that I'm never coming back. You deserve to be with someone who wants what you want. I can't be what you want. The only thing I can promise is that I'll leave you alone, forever.

I stood abruptly, grabbed my communicator, and smashed it into the screen.

"Miss Channing, sit down!" the officer scolded me.

"I don't deserve this." I paced the room. I felt caged. I was suffocating. "I trusted him. I believed him even when everyone said not to and he promised me we had a future, and now he's promising I'll never see him again. That's the furthest thing from what I want."

"Sit down." The officer closest to me grabbed my arm and directed me back to the chair. "We still have a lot to discuss."

"There's more?" I asked, taking my seat. How much more could I handle?

"You have no idea where he went?"

"No."

"When did you see him last?"

"A few days ago. He was going to another unit with his step dad."

"You haven't heard from him?"

"No." I thought that was pretty obvious.

"We picked him up on surveillance making his way to the Sweeper unit but we've yet to locate him."

That's not where Leon's family was. "What will you do when you find him?"

"You aren't privileged to that information. All we can tell you is that if he chooses to stay a Single, he can. Unfortunately, his poor decisions and actions affect you more than him."

"How so?" My emotions went from rage to fear.

"We don't have any pairing options for you."

"Garrett's been paired?"

"Yes."

"Pair me with Chance. He was my third option, he'll do. We can make that work."

"Chance has been paired and has relocated to Headquarters. He's not available. Braiden was your pairing and now that he's gone, that leaves you as a Single."

"Forever? I have to move to the Sweeper unit?" Thoughts scrambled my brain.

"Headquarters decided it'd be best for you to stay in your home unit and start training here. You already have a lot of knowledge so it doesn't make sense to move you, yet. It'll give you a year to work things out with Braiden, if we're able to locate him or potentially find you a new pair. The odds are against you, but given the circumstances, it's the best we can offer. Do you understand? Do you have any questions?"

"What's next?"

"We'll move you into your own housing unit and start basic training. When the year is over, we'll reassess where you are and take the necessary action at that time."

"Okay." I had to agree because I had no other option.

"We'll drive you home and explain this to your parents as well."

I was still in shock. My brain didn't want to process this information. My whole plan had failed. I didn't have Braiden or my new unit, and the pressure was now on to avoid becoming a Single. He promised to never be like his father, yet he fell right in line and did exactly what was done to him.

****

I sat on the couch next to my parents, fiddling with my new communicator. The Enforcers had just left, and I could tell my parents were still trying to process everything they'd learned about my upcoming year.

"Say something, please," I begged my parents.

"If I find him, Krissa. I'll kill him." My dad was serious.

"Dad, stop. I'm at fault, too."

"How do you figure?"

"I put myself in that position. I brought a lot on myself."

"I'm sorry you had to go through all of that, Krissa. I really wish you would've talked to me about it when it happened." He was now aware of the pregnancy and the turmoil that followed.

"I should've told you, I'm sorry."

"Yes, you should have."

"Don't blame Mom, I begged her not to say anything."

"Krissa, are you okay? Are you coping with everything that's happened to you?" My dad was at a loss. I could tell he was distraught over everything that had happened to me.

"I'm doing my best."

"Maybe you should go see someone. Go to counseling."

Yeah right. There was no way I could face Grace. I couldn't reveal all my heartache and secrets to her. Her son was the root of the problem. "I can't do that. I need to work this out on my own." I stared at my parents both looking like they'd just seen a ghost. "I'm going to go lay down, I'm exhausted."

"Krissa, it'll work out, I promise," my dad reassured me. "I'll never let you be a Sweeper. This is obviously for the best. Braiden was clearly never a good option. You deserve better."

In the days following, I semi explained what had happened. *He was gone and I was okay, it was for the best.* I knew everyone could tell I didn't think it was. I had several offers from my male friends to hunt him down and kick his ass, and while I did want him to physically hurt, I wanted him to feel the emotional pain I felt.

If there was a switch to turn off my love for him, I would've flipped it. I wasn't ready for a new relationship, but I was ready to stop hurting. I wanted to forget everything about him, but that was hard to do when everything around me reminded me of him. Restaurants we'd eaten at, movies we'd seen, songs on the radio. I couldn't escape my feelings or our memories.

****

"How are you doing?"

"I'm doing all right, Honor."

Honor, Hope, and I sat on Hope's bed taking a break from packing up her room.

"I still can't believe he's gone," Hope stated, obviously still in shock over my situation.

"I think this is going to be the best thing to happen to you. I can't wait for you to meet a guy that might actually be good for you." Honor draped her arm around my shoulders.

"That would be nice." I tried to sound enthusiastic and optimistic, but it felt so wrong.

"You still love him, don't you?" Hope didn't understand.

"I do." They weren't shocked by my answer, just confused and slightly appalled.

"Why?" asked Honor.

"Why do you let him get to you like that?" Hope asked next.

I didn't expect them to understand without knowing our history. "We just went through so much, it's hard to grasp he really left me. It's just so complicated."

"Like how?"

"If I tell you guys this, it can't leave here." If I didn't have their full attention before, I certainly did now. They pulled themselves closer to me and listened intently. "Promise?"

"Promise," they said in unison.

I wasn't sure why I chose to tell them. Maybe I was sick of trying to defend myself, tired of justifying my love for him.

"Our relationship was anything but average. This is really hard for me to talk about, so bear with me. Around Christmas I found out I was pregnant."

"What?" Hope said, mouth falling open.

"Oh my God. Why didn't you tell us? We knew something was wrong, but we never guessed that."

"I know. I just couldn't tell anyone." That's how our unit was. If anyone found out, it would've spread like a wild fire. I didn't want that, nor could I have handled that.

"What did you do?" Hope asked, still in shock.

"I lost the baby."

"Were you going to keep it?" Honor asked. I looked at her, surprised by the question, but decided to answer. I saw no reason to hide anything anymore.

"No. Not exactly by choice, but that's really the only option I had."

"I can't believe you went through that." Hope was still in disbelief.

"Me neither."

"Did it hurt?" Honor continued with the questions.

"Yes, but I think I'm more emotionally scarred than anything."

"What did Braiden do when he found out?" Honor allowed her curiosity to continue.

"Freaked out. He didn't really know what to do."

"He didn't want you to keep it?"

"No. He did not support me keeping it." I wasn't trying to make him out to be the bad guy in all of this, I wasn't trying to play victim. I was also going to tell them the truth.

"How did you guys do it?" Hope asked. "How did you not fall apart?"

"Well, I guess we did," I answered. "It was like after that, I needed him. I knew I wasn't strong enough to lose him, too. I was clinging to the only thing I had left. The automatic pairing freaked him out and it pushed him into something he wasn't sure he wanted. He never believed in the system and wasn't sure about it myself, but I accepted it. That situation dragged me through hell and back, yet I don't know if he's thought about it once since I lost the baby."

"I'm so sorry, Kris. I had no idea."

"Yeah, Krissa, you should've told us earlier. Maybe we could've helped."

"Thanks guys, but I didn't want to involve you. I wanted to fix it myself. Obviously, I didn't do such a great job. "I'd tried so hard to keep my emotions bottled up, but a few tears left the lower brim of my eyes.

"What a dick," Hope added.

"He did his best," I tried to defend him.

"No he didn't, Kris. He had no repercussions to his actions. It's not fair that you get everything dumped on you. That isn't right."

"That's just the way it is." I shrugged my shoulders. There was no changing it now.

"Have you heard from Chance?"

"No. He was paired and moved to Headquarters."

"That's probably for the best. He wasn't good for you either."

"I know. I'm just pissed that every choice has been made for me. If Braiden wanted to stay a Single, I should've known." Maybe I would've changed my picks. Maybe I would've had a chance to move to Headquarters. Maybe all of my dreams wouldn't have been ripped away.

"It'll get better," Hope insisted.

"I hope so." It felt better to have their understanding, but the burden was no different. It didn't make me feel better about my past.

Twenty Two

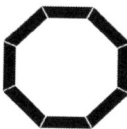

We stood in the middle of my new living room, surrounded by boxes that had yet to be unpacked. The place was quaint but I still needed to add a lot of personal touches. A part of me was hesitant because I knew my stay could be short lived.

"Mom, stop that!" I said, hugging her tightly. "I'm only ten minutes away. You can come visit me whenever you'd like. I love you."

"I love you too, sweetie. Call me when you're all settled in." I glanced around, sizing up my new place. I had a small living area that was connected to the kitchen with a small eat-in area. It was furnished, but not to my taste. I accepted that this would be my new home but it felt empty just like me.

"I will, Mom. Thanks for everything." I hugged my parent's good-bye and realized for the first time in my life, I was on my own.

"Wow, you've gotten a lot done," I told Farrah as I peeked into her apartment and saw all of the work she'd already accomplished.

I met Farrah earlier in the day as we both moved in our belongings. She approached me as soon as I passed her door, introducing herself the first opportunity she had. She was moving from the Agriculture Unit, her number one pick.

I walked into a replica of my space and tried to get to know her better. "Hi again."

"Glad you came back. How's it going over there?" She nodded her head toward my apartment.

"It's going, I guess. I still have a lot to do."

"I need to work on my closet." She brushed her long, black hair off of her shoulders. I looked over Farrah once more as we conversed; she was average looking, medium skin toned with a face full of freckles.

"I need to work on everything," I told her, looking back toward my apartment.

"I really haven't unpacked anything." I headed for the doorway. "I should get started. It was nice meeting you today."

"You too. We should get together sometime."

"I'd like that." Farrah picked up a pen and wrote her communicator number on the first thing she found. "Get in touch."

I took the paper from her. "Okay, will do," I answered as I left.

I could do this. I had to do this. As I stood in the middle of my empty apartment assessing my situation, it was comforting to still be located in my unit, but I felt so lost. How was I so unsettled in such a familiar place?

My first week of training went smoothly, nothing too difficult considering I wasn't specializing in anything yet. As for the new job, I was a little nervous because I'd never worked a day in my life. I was placed in one of the few clothing stores in our unit, and I found the job a relief from my real life. The computer system was simple enough and the inventory that came once a week was easy to sort through.

"Any plans for tonight?" Katie, the store manager, asked. Katie was a few years older than I, a little taller, with short, dark hair, brown eyes and full lips.

"My new neighbor wants me to go to a work party with her."

"Are you going?" she asked as we stood behind the wooden countertop, her checking the store's numbers.

"I might."

"You should. You deserve to have some fun." Katie would say that, she never missed a party.

Sighing, I leaned over the counter and rested my head in my hands. "I know I should."

"Why don't you head home and get ready. We're dead."

"You sure?"

"Yes, go."

I glanced around the empty store and gave in. "Okay, I'll talk to you later. Bye."

"Bye, Krissa, enjoy yourself."

"I'll try."

I was really making the effort to forget my problems, so I

figured mingling wouldn't hurt. I tried to keep myself preoccupied with work, school, and hanging out with friends, but nothing replaced the emptiness Braiden left behind. I was willing to try anything to divert my attention away from him. As I walked home, I pulled my communicator out and sent a message to Farrah confirming my attendance.

****

"Krissa, you look great," Farrah told me as I exited my apartment.

"Thanks."

We made our way through the house and I immediately knew I was out of my element. Boys were doing keg stands and playing beer pong while girls in their skimpiest outfits tried to gain attention. I missed my friends. An hour into the party, I was ready to go.

"Hey, Krissa," Farrah said, pushing her way through the drunken crowd.

"Hey."

"You're not into this, are you?"

"No, it's not really my scene. I don't know anyone here."

"That's the point. It's a great time to meet people."

"I guess." I shrugged my shoulders. I looked around, trying to see what Farrah saw, but it only cemented the thought that I didn't want to know these people.

"I'm going to go fill up. You good?" she asked, pointing to my cup.

"Still good." I showed her my full cup.

"All right." She pushed her way through the crowd of intoxicated co-workers.

I made my way up the stairs to try and locate another bathroom. I wasn't in the mood to wait in a long line, listening to obnoxious drunk conversations. I found one up the stairs, down the hall to the right. The sight of the bathroom's condition made me think twice. Carefully, I squatted over the toilet not touching anything for fear I'd catch some disease in this germ-infested area.

"Hold on, someone's in here. I'll be right out," I yelled when someone banged on the door.

After washing my hands and giving myself the once-over in the mirror, I opened the door to a drunken boy making his way into the bathroom. "Hey, sorry," he exclaimed. "I thought it was one of my housemates in here."

"It's all right."

"Hi. I'm Neil."

"Nice to meet you. Krissa." I took the hand he extended.

"Having fun?" he asked as he checked himself out in the mirror.

"Yeah," I finally answered.

"You're not a very good liar. Are you new to the area? I just got placed here."

"No. I'm from this unit."

I wasn't sure what else to say. We were standing in the

middle of a filthy bathroom and my encounter with Neil wasn't making my night any better. He was cute, but definitely not my type. He spoke with confidence that made it seem like he'd been around the block a few times.

"Well," I said, making my way toward the door, "I'll let you have your bathroom."

"Wait," he stepped in front of me, "I don't want you coming to one of my parties and not having a good time. What kind of host would I be?" He closed the door behind him. I heard the lock click and fear swept over me.

"Thanks, but my friends are waiting for me downstairs." This was the kind of situation I'd always been warned about. You never wanted to be in a circumstance like this. Nothing good could come from being locked in a bathroom with a strange, intoxicated male.

"I'm sure they'll understand," he said, sliding his hands up the sides of my body. Braiden's face flashed through my mind as Neil's unwanted hands continued exploring my anatomy. This was Braiden's fault. I just wanted to forget him for one night and this was where I ended up. If we were still together, I would have never been put in this situation.

"Stop!" I yelled, shoving him across the bathroom.

Apparently he wasn't used to rejection. "You stupid bitch!" he screamed at me, and then charged toward me. He grabbed my arms so hard I winced, then pinned me between his body and the door. He started kissing my neck and I could smell his stale beer breath. "I know you want it."

No, I definitely didn't want it. The only thing I wanted was to be out of there. I'd only have one chance to make my escape, and I planned to do everything I could to get out. As he reached for his zipper, I caught him off guard. I pushed him away as hard as I could and with everything I had inside of me I kicked him in the groin. I was full of rage. The kick was for him, for Braiden, and everything else that was fucking up my life. He dropped to his knees and I took the only opportunity I knew I'd have and fled the bathroom.

I raced down the stairs, found Farrah, and told her I was leaving. I didn't wait around to hear her reasons to stay. I didn't care. I wanted out of there, I wanted away from it all.

After my first, and last, adventure with Farrah, our friendship quickly came to a halt. She didn't believe me when I told her about Neil. Apparently, my encounter with Neil was a hot topic. Supposedly, Neil was gloating that I attempted to get with him and he'd rejected me. When he turned me down, I was pissed so I kicked him in the balls. Yeah, right. That was almost how it went down. I defended myself at first, but then decided to let her think whatever she wanted. She believed he'd never do something like that. It wasn't hard to avoid her because we worked on opposite schedules. She slept all day while I was busy at training classes or work and then partied all night while I was fast asleep. She was never going to make it in our unit.

On a few occasions I'd see Honor and Hope but sometimes it

was so hard to be around their happiness. Of course, I was happy for them and was glad it was working with their significant others, but at times it twisted my heart to witness it. I was embarrassed where my life was at and I didn't want to share it with them. I felt as if I had nothing in common with them anymore.

I did what I had to do to stay afloat. I had to keep up the appearance that I was on the mend and had to show that I hadn't lost interest in life. Everything I did was to save face. No one needed to see my interior deteriorating.

Twenty Three

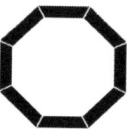

Two months into my new life and I still just existed. Air still moved in and out of my lungs, my heart was still beating, broken and all. My life was average as there was nothing special about it, no one to share it with. I was hoping time would've lessened the pain and help me forget, but instead, all that time made me miss Braiden more.

Katie invited me to a costume party her friend was hosting. I was hesitant considering the events that transpired at the last party I went to, but I trusted Katie. She and I had become close.

I figured this party was a good way to show I was still doing everything in my power to keep myself up and running. I may not have been happy on the inside, but nobody saw that. They saw a girl smiling, only they didn't know it was fake. They heard me laughing, still they didn't see the tears I shed. People only saw my façade.

"We're so dead today. Why isn't anyone out shopping?" Katie said, commenting on the store's lack of customers.

"Everyone is probably out already celebrating Halloween."

"Are you excited for tonight? Our outfits are so cute." She was dressing up as a sexy witch and I as some mystical fairy creature.

"Yes. They both came out great." She was more excited about playing dress up than I, but I was willing to go along with anything that would provide a distraction.

"Is Caleb coming tonight?"

"No, he didn't want to go. He's not big on socializing."

Caleb was her pair, her third choice.

"Do you think the pairing system works? Are you happy with your outcome?"

"I think it suits me fine. Caleb is a good guy. We make it work."

"Yeah, but are you happy?" I knew the question came from left field but Katie was an open book.

"I am."

"Even though he wasn't your number one choice?"

"Yes. We'd been friends for a long time, we knew each other well. I'm glad that we'll be together the rest of our lives." She was so sure of her future; I wondered what that was like.

"I'm nervous about what's going to happen to me. What am I going to do if Braiden doesn't come back? What if I don't find another pair? What if the system doesn't work for me?"

"Krissa, you just have to believe it'll all work out."

"I can't stay a Single. I don't want that life."

"You need to put yourself out there and find a pair. Good

thing we're going to a party tonight. It's a perfect place to meet new people."

"I guess." I wasn't optimistic about that. I knew most of the people in our unit and most were already paired. How was I ever going to find my mate? "I'm going to the bathroom, I'll be back. Do you think you can handle this all by yourself?" I asked, joking about our non-existent shoppers.

"I think I can handle it."

"Okay." I walked through the deserted rectangular-shaped store, fixing hangers as I passed. When I reached the dressing room, I heard one of our communicators beeping.

"Krissa?"

"Yeah?" I yelled from the back of the empty store.

"Your communicator is going off."

"Who is it?"

"It doesn't have any identification."

"Can you answer it?" I asked as I made my way back toward the front.

"Hello? No, this is Katie." I heard her confusion as I approached.

"Who is it?" I whispered.

She had a perplexed look on her face as she passed me my communicator. "It's Braiden."

To Be Continued ...

Torn True Love

About the Author

KD Ferguson, an avid reader and lover of fashion, graduated with a bachelor's degree in Fashion Merchandising. She grew up in Oneonta, NY, and currently resides in Concord, North Carolina with her husband and two rambunctious young boys. After several years of dipping her toes in the retail world, she is debuting her first novel, Torn-True Love.

@kristend732

http://adayinthelifeofkferg.blogspot.com/

Made in the USA
Charleston, SC
07 October 2014